The Story Babineaux

Mal Foster

First published in 2023 by PublishNation

This book is a work of fiction. Names, characters, and incidents are used fictitiously and are products of the author's imagination. Any resemblance to actual people, living or dead, is entirely coincidental.

Cover Design by Ritchie Cumberlidge
@ More Visual Limited

ISBN: 978-1-916696-25-9

By the same author:

The Asylum Soul

Fly Back and Purify

An Invisible Nemesis

Jude & Bliss

Fluke's Cradle

To Jules

ACKNOWLEDGEMENTS

Many thanks to Barbara Blow, Daniel Blow,
Simon Brown, Jude Browne, Joan Calder, Paul Clark,
Emma (Star Elizabeth) Foy, Rosalind Hill-Watts,
Paul Jackman, Jane Johnson, Pat Leeming,
Ola Napier Šatánková, Helen Naughton, Janette Prowse,
Jeannette Sale-Smith, Sue Stocker,
Nicky Thorne, Janette Watson, Ivy West, and Jan White
who I am aware have read all my novels so far.
Your continued support and honest feedback are greatly
appreciated.

Special thanks to Zoe Hatfield

AUTHOR'S NOTE

I started my writing journey when I was still in my teens. It was then I was advised by an old acquaintance to "write what you know." That statement is invaluable and one which has always served me well. Now though, I think it's time to perhaps be brave and cross the line, even question the limits of my own peculiar frailties. We all come to that point when imagination, fuelled by our inevitable selection of life's *what-might-have-beens* is just as important as reality. Writing fiction allows an author to often live their dreams (and nightmares) through their protagonist(s) and that's really what I've attempted here. I hope you enjoy the read.

ABOUT THE AUTHOR

Mal Foster was born in 1956 and grew up in Camberley, Surrey before moving to the Woking area in the late 1980s. He is a former local journalist and a widely published and award-winning poet. Now semi-retired, he is an avid fan of progressive rock music but turns to the late Canadian singer/songwriter and poet Leonard Cohen when pressed about who and what inspires him.

www.malfoster.co.uk

"Be with me now, great warrior, whose strength depends solely on the favours of a woman." – Leonard Cohen

1

Four o'clock in the morning. Everything was dark. I looked down at the floor. I could just about make out the empty whiskey bottle from last night's one-man pity show. I must have kicked it over in a crazy act of drunken defiance. There had been a power cut. When the electricity came back on—the hum of the central heating and a song on the hi-fi resumed from where my weary maelstrom of wild depression presumably left off at around midnight...

So darlin', darlin', stand by me - Oh, stand by me - Oh, stand - Stand by me, stand by me... A song that for some reason, has haunted me for most of my adult life.

Sue Grendel, a rather 'colourful' policewoman I was seeing, had walked out a few weeks ago. Apparently, she'd had enough of my drinking and so-called mood swings. 'I need to get my life back on track,' she said. 'Oh, and by the way, so do you!' she added.

I think breaking up with her must have been the root cause of my latest bout of depression. Apparently, even my subconscious obsession with Lianna, my ex, had all become too much for her. Pot calling kettle black in truth. Sue loved to sleep around, and I had known it from the off.

At first, it never bothered me, all I really wanted was the sex, rampant sex, but as my feelings for Sue deepened, it became a problem. Weird things happened that led to our initial frenzied love-making fizzling out until it was nothing more than 'a bloody awkward struggle' as she put it.

All that said I was now happy to be alone, so I couldn't understand why I had become so down. I knew I had to take a long hard look at myself and question my intentions, moralities, and weaknesses. I knew I should never have got together with Sue in the first place, but obviously, there was something about her. Something I couldn't resist.

The morning by now, was getting on, and the grey cloud outside had cleared. I stepped out into the fresh September air as a curious robin sang from a low branch in the laurel tree. I fed the fish in the patio pond.

Fortunately, things like nature give me hope and perspective. It helps clear my head. And in a way, it needed to. It was the day I was moving into my new office space to resurrect my career. Most of my working life I had always identified myself as being a journalist. Now it was time to move forward with some kind of purpose.

Two missed calls on my phone, both from Sue. I call back.

'Sue, you rang...'

'Hi Hun, I did. I just wanted to wish you luck. Have you moved into your new office yet?'

'Not quite, I'm still wrangling with the letting agency, but I expect to be in situ later this morning. I've been waiting for confirmation since yesterday.'

'Okay, give me a call when you're there. I'll come round after my shift. I have something I want to talk to you about.'

'Is it about us?'

'Does it have to be?'

'No.'

'But we are still friends, aren't we?'

'Good friends, I hope.'

'Of course. Look, I must go. I'll see you later.'

Now I was in a position of curiosity. I hadn't heard from Sue since we split at the end of July after just over a year together.

Getting ready to reinvent myself as a freelance reporter has been quite stressful, something I've always wanted to do but never had the courage to pursue. Having left the relative security of working for the Woking Tribune, this would always be a massive challenge.

My friends have told me it's one almighty risk, but hopefully, I can bite the bullet and prove them wrong.

Building a potential client-base for my reports hasn't been easy, but I have already set up a couple of channels with two other local weeklies.

I've always been a journalist, apart from a short stint at Sainsbury's as a shelf filler when I first left school in 1992. I was without any qualifications, but Binky Broomfield, the deputy editor of the Camberley Chronicle, who I met in a pub, offered me a rare apprenticeship for which I've always been grateful.

Now though, it's the hard part. It is finding the stories that will pay the grocery and energy bills. Where the fuck are they coming from?

Friends will probably say I should have thought about that before I walked out on the Tribune, but I had to take evasive action. Without a pay rise for over three years, mainly due to the Covid-19 pandemic and the paper's dwindling circulation, I was stuffed. If I'd stayed there much longer, I would probably have got the tin-tack anyway. I couldn't get along with the new editor, Tom Challis. He was such an arrogant, two-faced, and condescending individual! If you let him, he was one of those people who could get right under your skin. Things just weren't right.

Despite being a shy, bashful soul when I was younger, I now find it easier to speak to people, make conversations and hold my own. I'm also not afraid to make demands. I consider myself motivated, determined, and, most importantly, polite. The trouble is, it's always the bottle that gets in the way. My good friend Chris Larby even asked if I was cut out to go it alone. Too right I am. I know I'm thick-skinned enough to make this new chapter in my life succeed.

Journalism is something that generally doesn't pay too much. My earnings as a freelance will vary monthly, but others in the profession can make at least thirty grand a year. That's much more than I was getting at the Tribune. However, if I can squeeze a good living out of it somehow and enjoy myself at the same time, perhaps I will have made the right decision, no matter what Sue, Chris, and anyone else may think.

2

Two in the afternoon and Sue appeared. The first time I'd seen her since our split. There was something stern about her demeanour that I hadn't seen before. She looked different; her hair was cut shorter into a bob style, dyed ridiculously peroxide blonde but still showing her dark roots. Unusually, she was wearing heavy red lipstick. Her new look didn't suit her.

'Settled in?' she asked, looking around the office floor.

'Sort of, but I'm not happy. I think it's all going to work out to be quite expensive. I've signed a contract for a month. After that, I think I'll work from home. I only wanted the office address for the prestige. You know, business start-up ambition and all that.'

'Well, don't say I didn't warn you. You don't need to be spending on unnecessary overheads. I know you can't afford it!'

'Yeah, I know, I know. Anyway, what do you want to talk to me about? I assume you're okay?'

'Yes, yes. Apart from wanting to know how you are, there are two things.'

'Good things, I hope!'

'Well, maybe not all good. Not for you anyway,'

'Oh, thanks! Thanks, in anticipation.'

'I want you to hear it from me first.'

'What?'

'I'm seeing somebody. His name is Jim.'

'Jim?'

'Jim Green, he's a detective constable in the Met.'

'Another copper!'

'Yes, we met while liaising on a recent case. It was love at first sight.'

'Love?'

'Yes, love!'

I felt myself becoming angry. 'You told me you loved me once and ended up fucking everyone else in sight!'

'Please don't say that.'

‘Why tell me you loved me when you didn’t? That morning in bed, when you whispered, “I love you” in my ear, I thought you meant it.’

‘I did mean it. It made your ear go hard, didn’t it?’

‘Don’t try and be funny with me. It doesn’t work, and I find it quite offensive.’

‘Sorry, I must have been carried away. The “L” word can cause so much trouble, can’t it?’

‘And it has. Listen to me. It’s too late to apologise. Does this Jim bloke know what you’re like?’

‘Like? Like what exactly?’

‘Like a… oh, it doesn’t matter. You know…’

‘Are you calling me a whore?’

‘Promiscuous, maybe, and that’s me being polite.’

‘I told you what I was like when we met.’

‘I know, I know. I shouldn’t have gone against my morals.’

‘Morals? You patronising bastard!’

‘Why patronising?’

‘Because I think you’re a hypocrite. You were fascinated with me because I gave you great sex. I give everyone great sex!’

‘Now you are talking like a whore!’

‘Look, stop it. You’re upsetting me.’

‘Perhaps you had it coming. You can’t go on treating people like this, I mean, playing with their emotions. You should carry a National Health warning.’

‘You mean, like a cigarette packet?’

‘Something like that.’

‘Well, I’m not making any apologies. I like being who I am and doing what I do. It gives me fulfilment.’

‘What, sex gives you fulfilment?’

‘Of course, it does.’

‘And, what about the police?’

‘Being a police officer gives me fulfilment too. Are you done?’

‘We were done at the end of July. I’ve come to my senses since then.’

‘Give it a rest. Look, Mr Daniel Blue, we’re supposed to be friends. Why the constant bickering? It’s all history now.’

‘Sorry.’

‘Good!’

‘So, what else did you want to talk to me about?’

‘Oh, I almost forgot. Side-tracked. You can blame that on our trivial exchanges just now.’

‘Trivial. Ha, ha. So, what is it?’

‘I think I have a story for you to get your teeth into. I’ve been working on a case. The Chief Constable has ordered it to be dropped and put in the cold file. Problems with resources, as he put it. I was getting somewhere with this, and now the rug has been pulled from under my feet. I think you could unravel this and build a good story, but you’ll need to be discreet.’

‘How?’

‘Together with my intelligence, the reports I’ve compiled, and your investigative journalist skills, I believe you could get to the bottom of it. If so, the mystery would be revealed.’

‘Mystery, what mystery?’

‘You need to listen….’

‘I’m all ears.’

‘In 2012, a woman by the name of Virna Babineaux was murdered in London. She lived here in Woking at a house in Littlewick Road, not far from where you live in Knaphill. She was quite a famous glamour model back in the day, but as she got older, she turned to prostitution. She first came to our attention in 2009. We arrested her for running a brothel from her home in Knaphill. After her arrest, she branched out and opened new premises in London and across Surrey, including the terraced house in Roupell Street, near Waterloo, where we believe she was killed.’

‘Waterloo station?’

‘Yes.’

‘So, you don’t know who killed her?’

‘Actually, I do. Two men were arrested, with one eventually admitting to stabbing her twenty-one times. Both were banged up.’

‘Surely then, this is all done and dusted.’

‘It was. The killer, a guy called Robert Surcouf, committed suicide in prison about three years ago, and shortly after, his accomplice, William Kuznia, died of liver failure.’

‘That still doesn’t answer my question.’

'Virna Babineaux's body had laid unclaimed in the West London Morgue since her murder. No family or friends came to identify her. That is until a couple of years ago.'

'Then what?'

'A cousin of hers came over from Brittany, France. She contacted the police with concerns about Virna's welfare and wanted to know her whereabouts. She had walked into a police station in Lambeth, where they were able to find and out and tell her what had happened. Nothing more was heard. It later transpired the idiots had never kept any record of her name.'

'That's bad. Then what?'

'Mortuary staff later performed an audit on all the stiffs on their long stay list, and Virna's body was gone.'

'As in missing?'

'Yes!'

'No trace of it, no records, paperwork, nothing.'

'I thought if a body is unclaimed, it eventually receives a pauper's burial?'

'In normal circumstances, that would have been the case. Remember, Virna was a murder victim. Despite being stabbed all those times, results were inconclusive, and a second autopsy was recommended. I don't think that ever happened.'

'Have you contacted the morgue?'

'No, that's down to the Met, and that's where Jim Green comes in.'

'Oh, here we go….'

'Stop it! His report shows that hundreds of mortuary files were digitalised earlier this year from their original paper format. The mortuary assistant believes this was when any record of the body's second autopsy and subsequent removal may have been lost.'

'Am I right in assuming removing the body would have been a funeral director's task?'

'Yes, and by the way, that's not all.'

'What?'

'Virna Babineaux's house remains unsold. No-one has lived there since her death.'

'I expect it's probably a bit run down and overgrown by now.'

‘On the contrary, it’s still in perfect condition. But, as a neighbour tells me, no-one apart from a postman has visited.’

‘So, there must be piles of letters behind the door.’

‘Not at all. There’s a porch, and it’s visibly clear of any mail. Also, a vase of fresh flowers, geraniums or lilies is placed in the front room window each week. The curtains always remain partially open. As I said, the neighbour swears blind no-one has visited the house apart from the postman for the past ten years.’

‘Weird!’

‘I know. That’s precisely why I’m disappointed to have been pulled from the case.’

‘Obvious question. Couldn’t it be the neighbour playing tricks?’

‘She’s called Iona Turner, a former police sergeant. She retired from the Hampshire Constabulary in 2014. She said she was sixty-seven when I last spoke to her a few weeks ago. She’s quite a well-heeled woman. I’m certain she’s not messing with us.’

‘The name Iona Turner sounds familiar for some reason. I assume she has a key to this Virna’s house.’

‘Yes, she let us in during our investigations. Everything in the house is clean and tidy. No cobwebs or anything like that. It’s all very bizarre.’

‘There has to be a rational explanation.’

‘That’s what I believe… I think you should make a start by talking to Iona. Here’s the address,’ said Sue, handing me a torn-out page from her notebook.

‘Thank you! Actually, I’m pretty sure I was there many years ago. I think this lady used to be a friend of my mum’s.’

‘A good way to break the ice, then. Let me know how you get on. I want regular instalments.’

‘If I’m successful and get anything, I still need to submit to an appropriate outlet to publish the story. That’s the hard part!’

‘I’m sure it’ll all be good. Look, I must dash. I need to be back at the nick for a late notice four o’clock briefing. Oh, and good luck!’

‘Okay, bye.’

‘Take care of yourself, and don’t do anything I wouldn’t.’

‘That’s rich coming from you!’

Sue turned, smiled, waved, and hurriedly made her way through the reception and down to the ground floor.

3

Iona Turner's address is Tanglefoot, Littlewick Road, Knaphill, Woking. Indeed, it was an address I visited with my mum in the early 1980s when I was still a kid. A large pebble-dashed house set back from the road behind a row of ferns. When I arrived, some workmen were busy fixing a burst water main on the street outside. Before I could ring the doorbell, the front door opened. A very strict-looking woman with long grey hair tied back in a ponytail answered. I felt relieved when her expression broke into a big smile as she removed her maroon-framed spectacles and placed them on the top of her head.

'Ah, little Daniel Blue. My, how you've grown, my dear,' she said.

'What? You remember me?'

'Yes, dear, of course, I remember you.'

'You have a good memory. That must have been around forty years ago when mum and I used to come over on the No.34 bus from Camberley.'

'I must confess I do. Your poor mother, Dorothy, must have been gone quite a while now.'

'Yes, March 2004, it seems like only yesterday.'

'I hear you live in Knaphill now.'

'Yes, I moved into a house down the Broadway a few years ago.'

'Sorry, I didn't mean to pry. Tell me, why are you here? What can I help you with?'

'It's about the house next door to you. I'm a newspaper reporter now. DI Sue Grendel, who I think you know, suggested I pop around to see you for a chat. I was hoping you could tell me about the woman who used to live there. I believe you used to be a police officer too.'

'Yes, I used to be with the Hampshire Constabulary. I was based at Aldershot for the last few years of my career, Basingstoke before that.'

'Sue told me you were a police sergeant.'

‘I was, and it was no mean feat with all the male chauvinism at the time. I was very proud of those stripes, you know! That’s how I met your mum, at Aldershot, she was our canteen cook. We always had a good laugh in those days.’

‘It’s all coming back to me now. Mum always talked about those days with great fondness.’

‘And so do I. Look, come in. I’ve only just put the kettle on.’

Iona took me through to a backroom which had a large pine dining table. On one of the walls were photographs of what was clearly a distinguished policing career.’

‘That one of me, with her late majesty. It means so much to me now.’

‘I suppose it does. I was gutted when I heard the news last week. It was like losing one of my family members. It was the same sense of grief.’

‘I know. I still feel the numbness now. God rest, Queen Elizabeth!’

‘What’s all this?’ I said, pointing to a cork noticeboard on the opposite wall.

‘That’s my record of all the comings and goings. Well, at least the ones I know about. The postman and canvassers, that’s all. You said you wanted to find out more about the woman next door. She’s been gone over ten years now, you know. Virna Babineaux, her name was.’

‘Sue told me the poor lady was murdered in London.’

‘That she was, my dear.’

‘So, what about the house? What’s been going on?’

‘It’s all quite bizarre. Someone must be paying for its upkeep, you know, the mortgage, the council tax, and the utility bills. I mean, the water, electricity, and gas still work.’

‘Have you any clue who that might be?’

‘None at all, but one of the police officers suggested that Ms Babineaux had enough money in her bank to continue paying her bills.’

‘Even so long after she had died?’

‘Yes, she was quite rich.’

‘Then why did she go into prostitution?’

‘Only she will know. From what I gather, she was allegedly stripped of many of her assets by her killers. They couldn’t have got everything. Your police lady friend DI Grendel told me they were both quite stupid, and that's how they got caught.'

'So, Virna must have had a few bank accounts?'

'I didn't know her well, but she appeared quite intelligent. I guess she was careful with her money and didn't keep it all in one basket, so to speak.'

'Do you know how much the property is worth?'

'Houses around here all cost more than a million now. When she bought it in 2007, it would have been on the market for around £750,000.'

'Flipping heck!'

'Someone has been entering the property on what I think is a weekly basis, giving it a good clean and replacing the flowers in the front window. The problem is that I've never seen anyone leave or enter.'

'And the only person you've seen is the postman?'

'Apart from a few canvassers, yes, and any post is always taken away from the door. I think someone is hiding in there.'

'I assume the police have given it a thorough search.'

'Yes, I was naughty. I knew where the spare key was kept. I've had it ever since Ms Babineaux was murdered. No-one else should be able to get in. DI Grendel and her colleagues searched the house twice.'

'Did they look in the loft?'

'There is no loft as such. It's a large attic room. That was all quite new. There is lots of paraphernalia up there.'

'Paraphernalia?'

'Everything you might expect to find in a prostitute's dungeon, except it's upstairs at the very top of the house.'

'And the garden, that looks pretty well kept as well?'

'I can explain that. That is me. I pop around, give it a good weed, and mow the lawn as often as possible. At first, it was left alone for a couple of years and was like a jungle. Something was attracting the rats, so I decided to do something about it. After all, I have plenty of time on my hands these days. Finish your tea. I'll take you round there for a quick nosey in a minute. You might see something your detective friend and her colleagues may have missed.'

‘Thank you. Can I quickly look at the newspaper cutting you have pinned on the noticeboard?’

‘Of course, here. Please take it. It will explain the kind of woman she was. You’ll see it was from the Surrey Mercury in 2009.’

REPRIEVE FOR WOKING BROTHEL KEEPER

A Woking woman, and two accomplices who ran a number of brothels across the South, have avoided prison terms. Virna Babineaux (46), of Littlewick Road, Knaphill, was given a 12-month suspended sentence at Guildford Crown Court on Friday, 17 April, writes Stuart Searle.

Ms Babineaux and William Kuznia (39), and Helena Cieslak (40) all admitted to running a lucrative prostitute ring at the address near Woking.

The three defendants had their sentences suspended after the judge; QC Jennifer Dance, described their circumstances as ‘unique’.

Babineaux was given a 12-month prison sentence suspended for two years after pleading guilty to managing a brothel used for prostitution at her home at Littlewick Road, in Knaphill, Woking, as well as premises in London, Camberley and Aldershot.

She was also ordered to carry out 180 hours of unpaid work.

Kuznia was also sentenced to 12 months in prison, suspended for two years and ordered to carry out 120 hours of unpaid work for four counts of criminally acquiring property in connection with keeping a brothel.

Helena Cieslak of Roupell Street, London, received an 8-week term, suspended for 12 months, after pleading guilty to assisting in managing a brothel and acting as a maid at the premises.

All three entered guilty pleas after failing to succeed with a rare abuse of power case they had brought against the Surrey Police.

Babineaux and Kuznia were arrested when Babineaux made a 999 call after two men burst into the house on Littlewick Road.

The men were armed with what proved to be two World War Two German Luger pistols. Babineaux claimed a shot had been fired through a front room ceiling.

Surrey Police cordoned off a large stretch of Littlewick Road as they investigated the matter. A week later, Ms Babineaux and the other defendants were arrested on suspicion of brothel keeping following an extensive police investigation.

The court heard how Babineaux had told officers where her other brothels were as she believed the attackers were heading there, and she wanted to ensure the 'ladies' working in them were safe.

The court had also heard that Babineaux, a French national, had fallen on hard times after a successful modelling career fell apart in the late 1990s.

Sentencing Babineaux, Judge Dance, said: 'You were a keeper of brothels and made substantial profits from it. You must have been aware of the risks you were taking, and I suggest there should be no repeat. Your honesty with the police and what you have told the court has reprieved you all of a much heavier sentence.'

'The article mentions Roupell Street in London where Virna was murdered.' I said, handing back the cutting.

'The arrest of those three was a godsend. It meant that the neighbourhood's respectability was restored. Any outsider would never have guessed what Ms Babineaux was doing. She blended in well with the local folk when she was by herself. You know, nice hat, green waxed Barbour jacket and matching wellingtons. To anyone, she came over as a typical country girl, but as you know, she wasn't.'

'The article states that the court heard she had fallen on hard times. That can't be true.'

'I know it's not. As I've already told you, Ms Babineaux was shrewd. Someone has been working with supposition instead of fact. It's a common error made by inexperienced police officers and, further down the line, even barristers.

'Was she French?'

'Oh, definitely. The paper cutting says she was. From what I can tell, yes, but I believe she may have had a British father. If you go on your computer and play around on Google, you may find out more.'

'Oh, trust me, I will.'

'Okay, let's pop next door,' said Iona as she pulled on a black cardigan.

None of the houses in Littlewick Road has numbers, just names. At first, I couldn't see a name, but it was one of the houses I remember from when I was a kid.

'Here's the name,' said Iona pointing to a rose tree climbing up the wall. It's Mahraj.'

A branch of bright peach-coloured roses slightly obscured the name plaque.

On entry, we were greeted by a strong lilac smell.

'That'll be cleaning spray,' said Iona as she led me through the hallway. 'It's all very odd, isn't it?' she added.

'Yes, very. I notice a lot of paintings by the same artist around the house,' I said as I walked into the front room. 'Do you think they are originals?'

'Yes. Look, all by someone called Jonathan Blackwell.'

'I see. All pictures of ballerinas, clowns and naked women. Virna must have liked that sort of thing.'

'When the police were here, they took one of the pictures off the wall. They found an inscription on the back by the artist. Look, here it is,' said Iona, reaching to take one off its hook at the foot of the stairs.

To my darling Virna, all my love, Jonnie. *Fugazi.*

'Jonnie is obviously short for Jonathan, but what do you think *Fugazi* means?' I asked.

'I haven't a scooby,' said Iona.

I decided to look at all the other paintings; they all had the same message. In all, there were twelve of them.

'They are nice pictures, aren't they,' Iona added.

I walked into the front room and looked up at the ceiling for any evidence of a bullet hole which was mentioned in the article I had just read. Nothing?

'Come on,' said Iona, 'Let's look upstairs. I suspect you'll be interested in what's in the attic.'

'Flipping heck,' I said as I opened the door. 'I bet this room can tell a few stories.'

The room had everything. A low king-size bed, medieval stocks, a large cage, restraints, bondage harnesses, rope, black and red leather corsets, Pace uniforms, gimp masks, cat-o-nine-tail whips, nipple clasps and on the bedside table, scores of condoms symmetrically arranged on an old wicker tray.

'You look mesmerised by all the kinky gear,' said Iona.

'It's not quite what I was expecting, but then, I didn't know what to expect.'

'Someone is keen on keeping all this in place, and that's a big worry,' said Iona, smirking slightly.

'I'm sure it is, but why? Virna Babineaux is dead! There has to be an explanation. Did my friend Sue tell you anything about Virna's body?'

'No, dear, not at all.'

'Apparently, it had been lying in a morgue, unclaimed for years, and now it's gone missing.'

'What?'

'Sue and her colleagues have been taken off the case. The Chief Constable of Surrey Police dropped it. That's why she's alerted me. She hopes I can find something to help her reignite the investigation.'

'Oh, I see.'

'Do you think this artist guy, Jonathan, may have something to do with it?'

'I don't know. That's for you to find out. Perhaps you should consult your friend Google again and look him up,' said Iona, smiling.

'No doubt about that. I shall.'

'Just before we lock up, let's take a quick look in the garden.'

The garden consisted of quite a few apple trees and a bonfire pit at the bottom where some grass cuttings had been burnt, presumably by Iona. I also noticed a large concrete circle with an iron handle in the middle of the lawn.'

'What do you think this is?' I asked.

'I believe it covered an old well. I've tried to lift it before, but my lack of strength got the better of me.'

'Okay, let me try.'

Iona laughed as I failed miserably to lift the cover. 'Well, you won't be the next King Arthur, that's for sure.'

I laughed back but felt very embarrassed at the same time.

'Good luck with your search, young man. You know where to find me if you need anything else,' she said, smiling broadly as she shook my hand.

'Thank you, thank you for everything. I'll be in touch,' I said as I waited for what seemed like an eternity and watched her lock the front door.

As I walked home, I couldn't help but wonder if Iona was hiding something. Perhaps involved in some way. Sue had already told me she was kosher, but then that was Sue. What did she know? I think my next move must be to learn more about the artist.

4

A Google search for Jonathan Blackwell revealed only one post, which goes back to 2001. An article from the Southern Evening Echo shows him displaying one of his paintings at an art gallery in Weymouth, Dorset. The piece describes him as a talented and ambitious fifty-one-year-old. That, I thought, would make him around seventy-two now. If she had lived, Virna would now be fifty-nine, which fits with a twelve-year age gap. That's only relevant if they were romantically involved. Perhaps he may have been an admirer from her glamour model days. She certainly liked his paintings. The article states that he lived in Portland, Dorset, but doesn't pinpoint exactly where? Blackwell isn't a very common surname, so I should be able to find it quite easily on an electoral roll somewhere.

A search for Virna was much more interesting. Dozens of vintage photographs by a German photographer named Ros Muller showed her posing naked and walking through the streets of Pigalle, Paris.

Virna has a slender hourglass body, a long mane of curly blonde hair which reaches down to the top of a very well-shaped bottom, and her bust is phenomenal. Her expression is sullen with a classic model's pout. I can tell her lips are red. Sometimes, she's pictured close-up with an unlit Gauloise cigarette or cigarillo.

It's difficult to believe someone so beautiful would not be able to find something more lucrative than prostitution after finishing their modelling career. Though I suppose prostitution can be lucrative, it seems Virna had the class to make it work.

More information reveals that Virna was born as Veronique Guyot, the daughter of Nadine Guyot, a Paris housekeeper who died in 1998. Babineaux is a professional non-de-plume she had adopted in her late teens. Her father is recorded in legal documents as an unknown British writer. In another piece, Virna reveals she was the result of a one-night stand. 'I don't think my mother even knew his name,' she quotes in the article.

Ros Muller, the photographer, appears to have been quite famous in her day.

An easy Wiki search reveals that Muller was first recognised for her black-and-white photography of burlesque scenes and portraits of young females posing in leather and lingerie. By the late 1980s, she had switched to photojournalism and colour photography. It says her range of photographs explores strange and yet often simple worlds, locations, and situations.

She is described as a competent, precise, impartial, and sensitive observer. Much of her work deals with people living on society's edge, such as transvestites, strippers, prostitutes and the homeless. Her photos are always respectful and do not deprive any of her subjects of their dignity.

Another one of Muller's favourite topics is a fascination with sadomasochism. Again, Virna is pictured in a number of poses in what is presumably a dungeon.

In later days, Ros Muller turned to photographing mature and fully-clothed models for a Paris fashion house before her death in 2019.

Another quick scroll down in Google revealed a newspaper article from April 2013 by the London Evening Standard about the court case relating to Virna's death. I'm quite surprised I don't remember any of this from my time working for the Woking Tribune.

Virna Babineaux Murder – Killer Gets Life

Murder Assailant to serve a minimum of 25 years in prison after being convicted of stabbing a French prostitute to death at a London address in January last year.

The former model, Virna Babineaux, was murdered by Robert Surcouf, who was sentenced to life in prison at the Old Bailey in London on Thursday, writes Ruth Mayer...

The Staines man has been jailed for a minimum term of 25 years after stabbing a prostitute no less than 21 times to death, concealing her body and spending the money from her credit cards.

Surcouf, 41, of Hythe Road, Staines, Surrey, was sentenced for the murder of Ms Babineaux after a jury had convicted him on Wednesday.

Ms Babineaux, 49, died at a rented address in Roupell Street near Waterloo Station in Southeast London, where she operated as a 'mature escort'. Her body was placed in a large case and dragged to a decommissioned London taxi. The car was initially stored in a Southwark carpark before being driven to a location at Raynes Park, Southwest London until it was drawn to the attention of police after a papergirl alerted them to a 'peculiar smell'.

Virna was said by a close friend to have been a very private woman of French descent who lived at a luxury home in Knaphill, near Woking, Surrey and worked as an escort following the collapse of her lucrative glamour modelling career in the 1990s. Police described her murderer as a sly confidence trickster, a man who set himself up to kill and strip Ms Babineaux of her assets, indeed, everything she had worked for all her life.

Surcouf and his 'reluctant' accomplice, William Kuznia, were arrested by police after an extensive forensic investigation at the Roupell Street property revealed traces of their DNA and fingerprints.

'It appears no attempt by either man to cover their tracks was made,' stated arresting officer DI Poacher of the Metropolitan Police in his report.

Sentencing Surcouf, Mr Justice Campbell said he had 'systematically targeted' Virna and 'left her body to decompose. The body was abandoned in what was almost public view, having been poorly covered up on the taxi floor by a bloodied hearth rug'.

He went on to say Ms Babineaux was stabbed 21 times, and the subsequent disposal of the body underlined the fact that Surcouf had a total lack of regard for his victim. Surcouf had described her as his best friend in a police statement during his arrest. Judge Campbell called him 'calculated, callous, and a complete menace to women'.

DI Poacher told the court, 'The murder resulted from an apparent argument about money. A diary found at the address suggests Virna regarded him as a friend and would often offer him her services for free'.

Judge Campbell added that it appears Ms Babineaux was a risk-taker, making her vulnerable to men such as Surcouf.

He said: 'For reasons only known to yourself, you calmly and collectively set about killing this woman and ultimately stealing her assets to feed your greed. You then took the necessary steps to ensure her body would not be discovered for a certain period.'

Judge Campbell added, 'Surcouf embarked on the comprehensive asset-stripping of this lady's persona'.

No family members or friends of Ms Babineaux were present in court for the sentencing. It is believed her parents are both deceased. The judge confided that there was no record of any siblings or offspring.

Judge Campbell then sentenced Surcouf to life with a minimum of 25 years in prison. He also sentenced him to six years for perverting the course of justice and six years for conspiracy to defraud, both of which will run concurrently with his life sentence.

His co-accused Kuznia, 48, was jailed for 12 years, six for perverting the course of justice by concealing the death, and six for conspiracy to defraud.

Judge Campbell said, 'Surcouf was hell-bent on committing the fraud'. He added, 'Kuznia, his reluctant sidekick, could have made things easier for himself by taking no further part after witnessing the murder, but greed got the better of him.'

The pair went on to spend Ms Babineaux's money on luxury hotels, drugs, gambling and exotic escorts. The court was told Surcouf had a serious long-term gambling addiction which had accrued thousands of pounds of debt. The judge added that Kuznia was in the house when Surcouf murdered Ms Babineaux and was involved with concealing her body and spending her assets.

Judge Campbell added, 'The concealment of Ms Babineaux's body became a job for two people. Indeed, two individuals, simply motivated by greed. The whole operation was carried out with pure evil. According to the records of their previous convictions, both men have an appalling history of offences relating to dishonesty and crimes against women.'

In closing, the court heard that 15 months after the murder, authorities had so far been unable to release Ms Babineaux's body for burial or cremation, and her remains were still unclaimed in a London mortuary. A situation that an animated Judge Campbell told the court was 'scandalous!'

Neither man showed any emotion as they were taken down after the sentencing.

I remembered Kuznia's name from the Tribune article Iona had shown me. As Sue told me, both men are dead, which is such an irony. I feel, somehow, they've escaped their punishment.

After phoning Gary Stirling, one of my former colleagues at the Tribune, he reminded me I was bogged down with another story at the time involving the subsequent arrest of Mad Ted Harvey, a notorious gangster and local drug dealer. He was once the scourge of Woking, and the story was my first headliner for the paper.

Looking back, it now appears both stories were being run concurrently, which is how I somehow missed the Virna case.

5

My next move should be to visit the West London Morgue and learn more about the missing body's circumstances. A quick train ride from Woking to Wimbledon and then a District Line train to Hammersmith should get me there by lunchtime. The morgue is not too far from the Hammersmith Apollo, so I know the area quite well, having been there for gigs in the past. It's where I went with my old dad to see his one of his favourite bands, The Pogues, about a year before he died.

On entering, I noticed the mortuary building had its own unique surgical smell, something I hadn't experienced before. Everything was very bright. A young woman with shoulder-length brown hair, sunglasses perched on her head, a blue sweatshirt, jeans, and red shoes came out from behind the reception desk.

'Can I help you, Sir?'

'I hope so. I'm investigating the removal of a body.'

'Are you a policeman?'

'No, I'm a reporter.'

'Who with?'

'No-one particular. I'm freelance.'

'Oh. Wait, sit over there. I will need to get the manager.'

'Okay, thanks.'

The silence was almost deafening except for the clock, which reminded me of my one at home… Tick, tock, tick tock. After around fifteen minutes, a tall woman with scruffy blond shoulder-length hair, piercing blue eyes and a white coat appeared.

'And you are?'

'I'm Daniel Blue. I'm a reporter.'

'Reporter of what?'

'Reporter of stories, I hope.'

'Oh, Mr Blue, you have a sense of humour.'

'Well, I try, although many people I know would say otherwise.'

'I'm Juliet Edgar. I'm the Senior Forensic Pathologist here. What exactly can I help you with today?'

'To put it simply, it's about a missing body. The body of the late Virna Babineaux.'

'I suspect the same one a policeman was asking about a few weeks ago.'

'I wouldn't know when, but I guess so.'

'Wait here. I will need to get some clearance to speak to you.'

'Oh, okay.'

The young woman behind the reception desk advised me to remain seated.

'These things take time,' she said.

'Do you know anything about the case?' I asked.

'No, I've only been here for a few weeks. I moved down from Glasgow.'

'Hence the Scottish accent!'

She laughed. Just then, Juliet Edgar reappeared.

'I've been trying to get hold of my boss, the coroner. He's apparently in a meeting and will be occupied for the rest of the day. Look, come with me. I will do my best to help you if I can. First, can you sign the visitors' book and fill in this form?'

'Of course, thank you.'

Juliet took me to a side room to the left of a long corridor. I felt a chill as we walked through a set of double doors.

'We get used to that; the low temperature from our freezers causes the chilliness. We have fifty-two units.'

'Units?'

'Yes, we can store up to fifty-two corpses at any time. We also have a large post-mortem examination room that needs to be kept chilled. The pathologists are working on three new admissions as we speak.'

'Sorry, I hope I haven't taken you away from your work.'

'You haven't. Now, can I have a look at the form… Daniel Blue, a freelance investigative reporter, was born on 17 December 1976, and you live in Woking.'

'Yes, that's me.'

'And you're a member of the National Union of Journalists.'

'As a freelance reporter, it's advisable. It also backs up my Press Pass and other credentials. In fact, they supply a lot of my necessary documents.'

'Tell me, Mr Blue, who do you write for?'

'Anyone who will take my stories.'

'Now you want to write about a missing corpse?'

'Well, yes. What can you tell me?'

'There are a number of factors, and I believe the police were given all the relevant details. By the way, who informed you about this incident?'

'The police.'

'Really?'

'Yes, it's part of a case the Surrey Police were investigating, but it's since been dropped. One of their officers tipped me off and asked if I could continue investigating. Firstly, it would help me write a good story, and if I was successful, it could help the officer I'm speaking about get the case reopened.'

'Interesting. Then, why should I help you? It could be to our detriment?'

'Because you come across as fair and amiable, and I believe you are professional.'

'Okay, okay. You've won me over!'

'What do you think happened?'

'Well, I don't think it was anything sinister. There were no break-ins, and I'm sure none of those proverbial body snatchers has visited us. The whole incident has been put down to a simple clerical error. When an undertaker collects a corpse, the yellow forms we exchange could have gone missing or not have been filled in at all.'

'Is it usual for this sort of thing to happen?'

'Not at all. The thing is, we can't pinpoint the exact day the corpse was removed. It could have been anytime over the ten-year period it was supposedly stored.'

'Yes, I know the body had been here for a long time.'

'We have one gentleman's body that has been here for nearly twenty-five years and is still part of an ongoing police investigation. Unless there is a request for a viewing, a further post-mortem examination, or release for a funeral, there is no need for the unit to be opened.'

‘So, it wouldn’t have been released for a pauper’s burial?’

‘Of course, usually, that would be the case. However, your Miss Babineaux was a suspected murder victim.’

‘My police lady friend, DI Grendel said something along those lines.’

‘Most of the corpses we take are usually murder victims, or suspicious deaths. We specialise in the dodgy ones. You have seen Silent Witness, haven’t you?’

‘Err, no.’

‘Really? However, on this occasion, the recommendation for a second autopsy didn’t come to light until the recent Metropolitan police investigation.’

‘The body was discovered missing a few weeks after an unarranged visit by a cousin. That’s when the police would have been informed.’

‘Did they sign the visitor's book?’

‘Yes, on the 25 March 2020, but the signature was unreadable.’

‘Did they leave an address?’

‘No, unfortunately not. I still don’t know if it was a man, or woman.’

‘Unbelievable! Even I can tell you that the cousin was female. At least that’s what I was originally told.’

‘How do you know?’

‘DI Grendel. She told me.’

‘I think I know why there may have been a lapse in our usual protocol,’ said Juliet as she reached anxiously for her computer mouse.

‘What?’

‘All our old paper records were being digitalised during that period. A project was started so that we could load data into our new Spectrum computer system for faster and better access. The young Scottish lady in reception has only just completed the task for us. Her predecessor was too slow and made some awful mistakes. Ultimately, the work pressure was getting too much for her, and she decided to leave.’

‘So, would the new system also contain autopsy reports?’

‘Good question. Let’s see. I’ll turn the screen around. You’ll notice I don’t use it very much.’

'Thank you.'

'Ah yes, Babineaux. I can see clearly from this, the initial post-mortem report. It also shows a second autopsy was recommended.'

'But never took place?'

'I assume not. There's no record of any second autopsy on here.'

'That fits in with what I've already been told.'

'Would you like me to read the original post-mortem report? You'll have to excuse some of the jargon.'

'Yes, please, thanks.'

POST- MORTEM / V. BABINEAUX
10/01/2012, 11:30 a.m.
West London Morgue, Hammersmith
By Victoria Musgrove MD - Case 2012 – 010/1

Summary of Preliminary Post-Mortem – West London Morgue
Name of deceased: Virna Babineaux
White Caucasian/Female
Body Identified by: Helena Cieslak (Friend)
Police Case No. 0501/1001/Poacher D.I. - Police Force: Metropolitan
Evidence of Treatment: N/A

External Examination *The autopsy begins at 11:30 a.m. on 10 January 2012. The body was originally presented to WLM in a black body bag. At the time of examination, the body is wrapped in a clear, plastic film.*

Upon removal of the film, the body is clothed in a white button-down blouse, black skirt, and high black leather boots. A large bloodstain on the lower half of the blouse, and the material has multiple tears. The skirt reveals another smaller bloodstain, which appears to be the result of pooling blood and gravitational residual.

The body is that of a normally developed, well-nourished Caucasian female measuring 5 ft-7 inches in length, weighing 12.5 stone, and generally appearing consistent with the stated age of 49 years.

The body is cold and partially decomposed with developing Rigor-Mortis. Pronounced unblanched lividity is present on the lateral posterior of the body in the regions of the heels, legs, back, and arms and is pinkish in colour. Purplish lividity is also present on the posterior of the neck.

The scalp is covered by long, blonde hair, averaging 40 inches in length and has blue highlighting at the fringe that is consistent with cosmetic shop-bought hair dye. The body hair is female and average. The genital area appears waxed.

The skull is symmetric. The eyes are open, and the irises appear to be dark green. Upon further examination, the victim was wearing cosmetic coloured-contact lenses at the time of death. The victim's natural eye colour is blue, which corresponds with information obtained from the victim's French passport photograph. The eyes are symmetrically dilated and slightly cloudy.

The teeth are natural and well maintained with what appears to be some enhanced dentistry.

The anterior chest is of normal contour and is intact. The breasts are female and contain no palpable masses.

The abdomen is flat with visible multiple wounds consistent with stabbing (see below), and the pelvis is intact. The external genitalia are female and slightly protruding; there is no evidence of recent injury or abuse.

The back is symmetrical and intact with a series of wounds, again consistent with stabbing. The upper and lower extremities are symmetric, normally developed, and intact. The palms of the hands contain several incised wounds consistent with defensive wounds. The hands and fingernails have traces of blood.

There is a tattoo of a joker playing card on the left buttock. There are no additional residual scars, markings, or other tattoos.

. . .

'That's just the external part of the examination. Would you like me to carry on?' said Juliet.

'Yes, please.'

'Wait a sec. Daloney, love, can you bring us a couple of coffees?' she shouted to the receptionist on opening the door. 'Right, let's carry on. Are you finding this of any interest?'

'Yes, thank you. Very much so. Just one question, would you say the report is accurate?'

'One would hope so. Unfortunately, some of Daloney's predecessors appear to have lacked a basic command of the English language. What I'm saying is, things can get lost in translation.'

'Sorry, I don't understand.'

'The pathologist usually dictates their findings into a recording device. It's then transcribed into the format you see here.'

'Oh, I see.'

Internal Examination – Systemics

The brain weighs 1,317 grams and is within normal limits. The calvarium and base of the skull are normally configured and have no fractures. The dura is intact, and there is no epidural or subdural haemorrhage.

The skeletal system is unremarkable and is within normal limits.

The oral cavity shows no lesions. The mucosa is intact, and there are no injuries to the lips, teeth, or gums. There is no obstruction of the airway. The mucosa of the epiglottis, glottis, piriform sinuses, trachea, and major bronchi are anatomic. No injuries are seen, and there are no mucosal lesions. The hyoid bone, the thyroid, and the cricoid cartilages are intact. The lungs weigh: right, 358 grams; left, 357 grams. The lungs are unremarkable.

The heart weighs 214 grams and has an average size and configuration. No evidence of atherosclerosis or gross ischemic changes of recent or remote origin is present.

The mucosa and wall of the oesophagus are intact and grey-pink in colour, with no lesions or injuries. The gastric mucosa is intact and pink with no damage. No unusual stomach contents are found. The mucosa of the duodenum, jejunum, ileum, colon, and rectum are intact, with no injury or signs of abuse. The small intestine is ruptured and has multiple lacerations.

The kidneys weigh left, 109 grams; the right, 107 grams. The kidneys are anatomic in size, shape, and location without lesions. The pelvic-calyceal system and ureters are unremarkable. The urinary bladder contains 6 ml of clear yellow urine.

The structures are within normal limits. Examination of the pelvic area indicates the victim had not given birth and was not pregnant at the time of death. Vaginal fluid samples have been removed for further analysis.

Toxicology: Samples of central and peripheral blood, the vitreous, gastric contents, urine, liver, and bile have been submitted for toxicologic analysis.

Serology: A sample of right pleural blood is submitted in the EDTA tube. Routine toxicologic studies have been ordered.

. . .

'Virna was apparently stabbed twenty-one times. Are there details about the actual injuries?'

'Yes, right here. I hope you're not squeamish,' said Juliet with a big grin.

'Mm, thanks. I hope I'm not as well.'

Description of Injuries

There is a total of 18 stab wounds, all in the abdominal area. They are all predominately in the umbilical region measuring up to 5cm depth, 2cm, length.

A larger stab wound is evident on the abdomen in the umbilical region, approximately 4cm superior and 5.5cm lateral to the navel. The wound is slit-like and measures 4cm in length. The depth of the wound is approximately 8cm. Note: This is a possibly fatal injury but not 100% conclusive.

There are also several premortem defence wounds on the victim.

(1) A cutting or incised wound on the palmar surface of the right hand at the base of the index finger. The wound is 2cm in length. The depth of the wound is approximately 1.25cm. This is a non-fatal perimortem injury compatible with a defence wound.

(2) A cutting or incised wound on the palmar surface of the right hand just proximal to the web of the thumb. The wound is 1.25cm in length. The depth of the wound is approximately 5cm. This is a non-fatal perimortem injury compatible with a defence wound.

(3) A cutting or incised wound on the palmar surface of the left hand at the web of the thumb. The wound is 2cm in length. The depth of the wound is approximately 0.5cm. This is a non-fatal perimortem injury compatible with a defence wound.

Overall, most of the wounds suggest a single-edged blade,

although a double-edged blade cannot be fully discounted. It is suggested that whilst the killer carried out a frenzied attack on the victim, he/she did not have the required command of the blade to penetrate further into the body, leaving only a maximum 8cm deep incision. This incision did not penetrate any specific vital organ.

In summary, I doubt if any of the knife blows were sufficient to cause fatal injury and that death may have been caused by other means.

I declare my results are inconclusive and recommend that the Southeast London Coroner's Office orders a second autopsy.

See separate file for drug analysis - 2012 – 010/1/D

Medical Examiner: Victoria May Musgrove MD
Assistant: Dr Ian Hogarth
10 January 2012

. . .

'So, let me get this right, Virna was only really stabbed eighteen times?'

'Yes, the other three wounds were what you might call slashes. This is typical of a frenzied knife attack. Most pathologists will refer to each entry wound as a "stab" for the purposes of simplicity.'

'Would you say the measurements of the wounds are correct?'

'One would hope so. It's always difficult to tell. However, we do have specialist instruments to enable us to measure such wounds.'

'And, what about the drug analysis? What does that file say?'

'Hold on, I'm still looking for it,' said Juliet while frantically scrolling up and down with her computer mouse. 'Nope, it's not here. Wait there. I'll go to the old file room and see if the original paper copy is still there.'

By now, both our coffees were cold. After about ten minutes, Juliet returned.

‘No luck. Daloney’s confirmed that all the old files were shredded when the digitisation program was finished three weeks ago.’

‘That’s bad luck.’

‘It’s worse than that. It’s tantamount to criminal negligence. Without that file, the post-mortem is practically invalid. Victoria Musgrove should have recorded it all in the same report. I’m surprised the police never picked up on that.’

‘Can’t you ask her?’

‘Victoria Musgrove? I would if I could. Don’t forget this is all from ten years ago. She must have left a while ago. I’ve worked here for five years and never met her. The staff turnover here is generally quite rapid, though I’m not sure why.’

‘Well, thank you for all your help. Just one more question.’

‘What?’

‘What’s the difference between a post-mortem and an autopsy?’

‘Essentially, they are the same thing. A post-mortem is usually the preliminary examination, and we always refer to anything after that as an autopsy.’

‘Thanks, I’ve always wondered.’

‘Is there anything else I can help you with today?’

‘I don’t think so. You’ve helped enough already. I hope I haven’t got you into any trouble.’

‘So do I!’

I came away thinking about the missing drug analysis data. Juliet looked horrified when she realised it wasn’t there. Now, I have a dilemma. Should I contact Sue and tell her everything her fancy man, Jim Green, may have missed during his recent investigation, or do I keep schtum?

I also noticed from the report that her former maid, Helena Cieslak identified the body.

6

The more I investigate Virna's case, the more intriguing it becomes. I can't help wondering what happened to her body. Who took it? Has it been buried or cremated? Was her body taken by mistake? That would mean the wrong body was released for a funeral, and the intended corpse is still somewhere in the morgue!

I was also surprised that Juliet Edgar always referred to bodies as corpses. I would have thought that would have been disrespectful, particularly if family members were visiting.

I now had to consider my next moves. A visit to find the artist Jonathan Blackwell is on the list, but first, I would like to find out more about Virna, where she grew up, and where she did her modelling. I also need to visit the murder scene on Roupell Street in London, something I could have done yesterday after I had left the morgue. The problem is, I don't have a house number, but someone around there must know something, even after ten years.

Strangely, I used to go to school with someone called John Roupell, so the name stands out. Another of life's silly little coincidences, I suppose.

My first stop was the King's Arms pub to see if I could get any information on which house Virna's murder took place. After ordering a pint, I asked the barmaid, who appeared Eastern European.

'No, I don't know. I've only worked here for a month.'

Just then, somebody else appeared—a rather overweight guy about thirty, wearing an orange-coloured Hawaiian shirt.

'Hi, I'm the manager. What are you looking for?'

'Hello there, I'm a journalist. I'm doing a story on a murder which happened in Roupell Street about ten years ago.'

'I don't know anything about any murder.'

'Have you worked here long?'

'Two years.'

'Perhaps that's why,' I said.

'You could ask me,' said an old man who sidled up beside me at the bar. 'I remember it well. The whole street was shut off. There were police all over the place for a few hours.'

'You remember?'

'Of course, I do. I live around the corner on Theed Street. We had to walk the long way round to get to the pub. Most inconvenient it was.'

'Tell me more, oh, hang on, let me get you a pint.'

'Speckled Hen, please.'

'Sure, no probs.'

'It happened up the top of the road, the house next door to the old bombsite houses. They're the newer ones at the top of the street. They were built quite a while after the war. The original houses were all built around 1824. They were lived in by bakers, blacksmiths, builders, butchers, nurses, teachers and even the odd prostitute. Now it's all yuppies and bloody foreigners.'

'Tell me more.'

'At first, no-one knew a murder had taken place. I've since heard that the woman's body was removed in the darkness of night. The woman who used to live there was called Helen or something like that. We all thought it was her, but it turned out to be someone with a French-sounding name. It was all over the Evening Standard for weeks.'

'The woman who lived there, could her name have been Helena, Helena Cieslak?'

'Yes, yes. That's it, that's her. A couple of other women were always in and out.'

'And the French woman, was her name Virna Babineaux?'

'I think so, but to be honest, I didn't pay much attention. It was such a shock to find out there was a knocking shop at the top of the street.'

'Which house was it exactly?'

'You can't miss it. It's up there on the right. It's all boarded up with scaffolding around it. It's like a building site. No-one has lived in there since the murder.'

'What happened to Helena?'

'Now, if I tell you, you know that's going to cost you another pint,' said the old man removing his cap. 'By the way, who am I speaking to?'

'I'm Daniel. And you are…?

'I'm Alf. Just call me Alf.'

'So where is she?'

'Not far. She still lives nearby and works in the pub around the corner. The murder of her friend shook her up. She didn't want to live in that house anymore, and she moved into a flat.'

'Where's the flat?'

'Around the corner in Hatfields. It's in a big tower block called Styles House.'

'What number?'

'No idea, sorry.'

'So, which pub does she work in?'

'The Ring. It's on the corner of The Cut and the Blackfriars Road.'

'Thanks, I think I'll make that my next port of call.'

'I know the history of the whole area. If you've got time, I can tell you all about this part of town.'

'No, it's okay, thanks,' I said as I grabbed my jacket and made a move.

As I walked up Roupell Street, I could see the house Alf was talking about. The whole interior had been gutted. A couple of men were working inside, and on the road was a skip containing old floorboards, paint tins, and light fittings.'

I walked around the corner into Hatfields and noticed the block of flats where Alf said Helena lived. At the main door was a panel with about forty buttons. Not knowing the actual number, I thought I'd carry on walking until I reached The Ring.

Like The King's Arms, the pub was nearly empty. A woman, I'd say in her early fifties, was working behind the bar. Light brown hair with pink streaks, tied back, black polo shirt with pub logo and the word 'Staff' on her back.

'Afternoon, sir. What would you like?'

'Something strong. A double Jameson's, please.'

'£8.20.'

'Flipping heck.'

'Sorry, it's so expensive.'

'Don't worry. It's not your fault. In truth, I shouldn't be drinking.'

'Are you an alcoholic? We're not allowed to serve alcoholics.'

'No, nothing like that. Let's just say I let it get the better of me a few years ago. It did more to my head than it did to my liver.'

'Oh, I see.'

'You don't happen to know anyone called Helena, do you?'

'Yes, I'm Helena.'

'Helena Cieslak?'

'Yes.'

'I'm Daniel. I believe you knew Virna Babineaux.'

'Are you a policeman?'

'No, I'm a journalist.'

'Oh. Wait there.'

After a minute or two, Helena appeared with a much younger woman.

'Mara is going to cover me for a few minutes. I'm due a cigarette break now anyway. Let's go and sit outside.'

'Why are you looking for me?'

'Look, I know what happened with Virna and how she died. I also know about the profession she was working in and how you were involved, I've seen newspaper reports in which you were mentioned. I just want to know what Virna was like and if you can shed any further light on things.'

'I can't, and I don't think I should. Though, I can tell you that she was a lovely lady who didn't deserve to die. Robert, the man who killed her, hated her being on the game. She didn't need to be. He felt he owned her and followed her everywhere. He wanted a share of her money. He wanted everything.'

'Would that be Robert Surcouf by any chance?'

'Yes. They were childhood sweethearts growing up in Paris. When Virna started modelling, they drifted apart and then around about 2008, he turned up in England like a bad penny. He had nothing. Virna started to feel sorry for him. The more she gave, the more he took. In the end, the fucking bastard killed her.'

'Did you witness the murder?'

'No, I was back home in Poland staying with my Uncle Marek. If I were still in London, she wouldn't have died. That piece of shit wouldn't have dared to try and kill her while I was about.'

'Did you know Surcouf is dead now?'

'Yes, he got moved to a psychiatric hospital and slit his wrists with some broken CDs. Even that was too good for him.'

'Did you know Virna's body was lying in a morgue for quite a few years, and now, it's missing?'

'You're asking too many questions, but a policeman came a few months ago and told me the same thing. It's all very upsetting.'

'Sorry.'

'It helps to talk about it sometimes. Sometimes it doesn't,' said Helena, wiping a tear from her eye.

'Do you have any ideas about who might have taken the body?'

'No. I do know one of her cousins came looking for her, but that's all.'

'Do you know the cousin's name?'

'No, sorry. But I can tell you all her close cousins were women. Two lived in Paris, and one, somewhere else, Brittany, I think. that's all I know. There were three of them altogether.'

'Are you sure you don't remember a name?'

'Yes, absolutely. Virna and I were good friends, but she didn't tell me everything. I don't think she ever told me any of their names, if she did, I can't remember them.'

'Okay, thanks.'

'Look, I have to go back inside now. Enjoy your whiskey.'

'I will.'

I was surprised Helena spoke so openly but thought she may have been a little economical with the truth. Something didn't feel quite right about her.

7

In all the excitement about the case lately, I had forgotten I had an important doctor's appointment. My blood pressure was up, and my libido was down. I knew I had to do something before my sex life suffered even more. It didn't help when Sue left. There was no-one to have any sex with, so I was unsure of my current sexual capabilities.

More stress and uncertainty. And now, a lack of self-confidence was affecting me even more. I felt I was sitting on the edge and afraid I might hit the bottle again. Big time!

I needed to get myself sorted. No more self-doubt, overthinking, and self-infliction. Hopefully, the doctor could help.

'Ah, Mr Blue, how can I help you? I'm Shana Suman.'

Just my luck. A replacement stand-in female doctor when I wanted to talk about my delicate manly things.

'Well, Mr Blue?' she said assertively, following my involuntary moment of hesitation.

'To put it in a nutshell, I'm suffering from a few issues which I think are affecting my sex drive.'

'Nothing to be afraid of. What does your partner say?'

'I haven't got one anymore. She left.'

'Were you together long?'

'No, not really, just a year or so.'

'Now, Mr Blue. What makes you think you have a problem?'

'To put it bluntly, it's not standing to attention anymore. I mean, not properly. It goes hard in anticipation, but when it comes to the point that matters, it suddenly droops like a French stick in the rain.'

'Oh dear! Do you masturbate?'

'Excuse me?'

'Do you masturbate? Come on. Tell me the truth.'

'Sometimes.'

'Look, it's nothing to be ashamed of. All men like a good wank.'

I laughed.

‘Come on. There’s no need to be nervous. Go behind the screen and drop your kegs. Let’s see if I can get you sorted.’

It wasn’t what I was expecting. I had to remind myself I was at the doctor’s surgery, not in a bedroom. The doctor was a very attractive, petite Indian lady. Very young. About mid-twenties, if that.

‘Well, Mr Blue,’ she said as she wrestled with a surgical glove.’ The penile shape is normal. You should be rather proud. However, your scrotum looks slightly on the large side. Excuse me while I have a feel around for any lumps. No, nothing to be afraid of there.’

‘Good.’

‘Pull up your bits. Let’s check your blood pressure.’

I walked back to the other side of the room and sat back in the chair by her desk.

‘Pull your sleeve up a little further, please,’ she said as she tightened the monitor pad around my arm.

At this point, I did feel nervous, perhaps sensing the reading was going to be high.’

‘Mr Blue, how old are you?’

‘Forty-five, I’ll be forty-six in December.’

‘Mm, 190 over 98. That’s rather high. Look, I’m going to upgrade your meds. I want you back here in a couple of weeks. If you continue to have high readings like that, you’ll be susceptible to a stroke or even a heart attack. You’re still a relatively young man. Perhaps you need to change your lifestyle.’

‘That’s what everyone says,’ I said, wondering what she would ask next.

‘Do you smoke?’

‘No, never have.’

‘Drink?’

‘Sometimes.’

‘Tell me the truth.’

‘Okay, a little more than sometimes.’

‘If you’re not honest with me, I can’t help you.’

‘Sorry.’

‘Your notes here tell me you’ve had a previous problem with alcohol.’

‘Yes, that was all about depression. I’m not an alcoholic.’

'Is that denial I hear in your voice?'

'No. Depression. It was depression. That's the truth.'

'It seems to me that you're currently living your life in a vicious circle. Here's what you need to do. Stop drinking.'

'Completely?'

'Yes, completely. Within a few weeks, your blood pressure should lower. You should then see signs that your libido is returning. It won't happen overnight, but if you follow my instructions, it will happen. Then, you should be confident enough to go out and find yourself a nice new girlfriend.'

'That's easier said than done.'

'Here, take this to the pharmacy. I've upped the dosage on a couple of your normal prescription tablets.'

'Okay, thanks. Is there any chance you could prescribe me some Viagra?'

'Sildenafil? No, absolutely not. That blood pressure needs to come down first. When it does, I will consider it. You need to keep your part of the bargain. Right?'

'Yes. Right!'

'I also want you to see the nurse for a blood test. Then, I can check you all over, you know, have a look at your sugar levels. I also need to see if you are carrying any signs of cortisol.'

'Cortisol? What's that?'

'Cortisol suppresses the amount of testosterone we all have in our bodies during stressful times. It happens to men and women. It usually occurs during an extended period of upheaval. Have you experienced any recent upheaval?'

'Where would you like me to begin?'

'Tell me! As I said, be honest. Perhaps I can help you!'

'My change of job. I've recently become self-employed as a freelance investigative journalist.'

'That's interesting. What were you doing before?'

'I worked for the Woking Tribune, but they didn't pay me enough.'

'Oh, I see. What else do you think has affected you?'

'Sue, my last girlfriend, her leaving me didn't help, but I like to think I'm over that now.'

'Do you still see her?'

'I've seen her once. It felt like she was haunting me.'

‘Sometimes a relationship break-up can be worse than grief. At least with death, we all have closure.’

‘Yes, and that’s what it still feels like.’

‘You definitely need to move on. Try and put the past behind you. Do you regard yourself as sentimental?’

‘Not really, but I have been labelled a “sentimental mercenary” before!’

‘That’s a new one. Don’t forget to see the receptionist on the way out and book an appointment for next week to see the nurse.’

‘Thank you. I will.’

I wasn’t surprised that my blood pressure was high. It always is. It has been since I was in my twenties. It didn’t help with such a nice young lady doctor looking me over. I’ve heard of white coat syndrome before, but I think this was different.

I liked what she said about finding a new girlfriend. Perhaps I should, but I’m getting too old, and the thrill of the chase doesn’t thrill me that much anymore. Those days are long gone. However, I do miss the sex. Giving up alcohol completely was going to be a massive challenge.

8

A few weeks had now passed since my visit to the doctor. I still hadn't stopped drinking. Cut down, yes, but not eliminated it. I wasn't doing myself any favours, and I wasn't sure why?

Sue had phoned a couple of days ago and asked how I was getting on with the Virna Babineaux case. I gave her an update but refrained from telling her about the missing drug analysis, which should have been part of the full post-mortem report. It was clear her fancy man, Jim Green, had almost certainly missed it when he was investigating the matter. No doubt Sue would have felt I was having a dig if I had mentioned it. I was also a little worried that if I said something too prematurely, the police would reopen the case, and all this would have been for nothing. That was perhaps one of my wiser moves.

It was time to settle my curiosity about Jonathan Blackwell. If I tracked him down, he might be able to tell me more about his relationship with Virna.

I had already discovered he was living in Portland, Dorset, in 2001. Would he still be there? It was a long shot, but one I felt was worth investigating.

Having taken the train down to Weymouth, I decided to look in on a few small art galleries in the town. After searching and studying some details on my phone, I found Calypso Fine Art Specialists on a side street a few yards from the seafront. I walked in.

'YES,' boomed a voice, seemingly out of nowhere.

'Oh, hello,' I said as a man, in his eighties, or even nineties stood up from behind the counter.

'Need any help?'

Despite his advancing years, the man was well-built and sprightly. I got the immediate impression he was the owner of the gallery.

'I'm looking for Jonathan Blackwell,' I said.

'WHO? Look, you need to speak up. I'm a little mutton and jeff, you know.'

‘Sorry, I’m looking for an artist called Jonathan Blackwell. Do you know him?’ I said a little louder.

‘I’ve got nothing of anyone by that name. I’ve got a seascape by Jonathan Weller. Would that be him?’

‘No, I don’t think so. This guy paints things like ballerinas, clowns, and nudes.’

‘No, my friend. We don’t exhibit that sort of stuff here. You could try Claire Broughton’s in Boleyn Crescent. She’s been there for years and will probably know who you’re looking for.’

‘Where’s Boleyn Crescent?’

‘Go to the top of this road, then turn right, and then right again. It’s not too far. It takes me about twenty minutes. You’ll probably get there in no time.’

‘Okay, thank you!’

When I reached Boleyn Crescent, I managed to confuse myself. It was a residential area with terraced houses—no sign of a shop anywhere. I walked up and down a couple of times and wondered if the old man had given me the wrong street name or was having me on. I was about to walk back to his shop and ask again when a woman about my age, wearing a blue denim jacket and red baseball cap asked if I was lost.

‘You appear to be a little lost, sweetie,’ she said.

‘In a way, I am,’ I said, reaching down to stroke her Rhodesian Ridgeback dog. ‘I’m looking for an art gallery called Broughton’s.’

‘Oh, Claire Broughton’s. Are you expecting to find a shop?’

‘Well, yes.’

‘Look, can you see that white house down there on the corner?’

‘Yes.’

‘Alongside, there is an alleyway. Walk past a tall monkey-puzzle tree and through a light blue gate. You will come to a ramshackle of a shed. It’s all part of the same property. You should find Claire in there. It is Claire you’re looking for, isn’t it?’

‘Yes, yes, thank you!’

Now I felt a little relieved and less confused. I managed to find the gallery quite easily. It resembled a wartime prefab, was set back a little, and was bolstered with rope and dark brown wooden slats to hold its decaying walls together. There was an array of dreamcatchers above the door. To enter the gallery, I had to brush aside several metal and bamboo wind-chimes which were hanging down which inevitably announced my arrival. I guess it was Claire's way of knowing she had a customer.

'Hello, is there anyone here?' I said as I entered.

Nothing.

'Hello!' I said again, this time a little louder. I was even beginning to think everyone around Weymouth's arty-farty land was deaf.

'Hello, sorry, just fixing a leak in the ceiling,' said a woman appearing from another room at the back. 'How can I help you?'

'I'm looking for a particular artist called Jonathan Blackwell. Do you know him?'

'Bugger me and blow me down with a feather. That's a blast from the past. Know Jonathan? Bloody hell, of course I know the old bleeder.'

'Flipping heck!'

'I haven't got any of his work here if that's what you're looking for. I haven't seen him in years.'

'When was the last time you saw him?'

'Fifteen years ago, at least. The last I knew, he was living in Fortunes Well, around the corner from the pub.'

'In Portland?'

'Yes.'

'Do you remember which pub?'

'The Red Star Inn. It used to be a crazy place, and the locals were all quite odd. Many are the descendants of pirates and smugglers. Go and have a look around. You'll find quite a few graves on the cliff top up there. Nearly all of them are marked Jon or John. It was a common name around here a few hundred years ago.'

'That's great, thanks.'

'Hang on, I'm trying to think of the name of the road, ah, Mallams, that's it. He used to live halfway down on the left. Don't ask me which number, though.'

'How well did you know him?'

'It's a long story. Jonathan was always what you might call a womaniser, you know, a ladies' man, and I'm the kind of woman who doesn't like sharing. Catch my drift?'

'Oh, absolutely.'

'Why are you looking for him? You don't look like one of the artist crowd.'

'Probably not, but I do like to know things, and I appreciate good artwork when I see it.'

'Have you seen any of Jonathan's art?'

'Yes. Clowns and ballerinas, you know, that sort of thing.'

'Nudes as well, no doubt.'

'Yes, and those.'

'Jonathan painted a portrait of me once. It looked nothing like me, of course, other people said it did. It was more of an abstract really. Oh, forgive me, would you like a glass of wine? I've got a nice bottle of Italian merlot on the go.'

'I better not. I've supposedly given up drinking.'

'Supposedly?'

'Doctor's orders, but so far, I've failed miserably.'

'Go on, have a glass. Let's raise a glass as a toast to your doctor!'

I laughed. 'Oh, alright then.' I said, submitting to Claire's charm.

Claire appeared to be in her late fifties. Greying corkscrew shoulder-length hair with a cheery, welcoming, almost permanent smile. She was dressed like a 1970s hippy with a long flowing dark green coloured psychedelic silk dress. I noticed she also wore brown sandals with silver bangles around her ankles. Her toenails were painted with turquoise varnish.

'I see you like the wine. Want some more?'

'Is it that obvious?'

'Don't worry. I have plenty more out the back. I usually get through the best part of a couple of bottles each day. I never drink on a Monday, though. I have one day off to prove to myself I'm not an alcoholic.'

'Sounds like a plan.'

'Well, something's working. I haven't been drunk for over twenty years. What about you?'

‘August 2017. I embarrassingly fell flat on the floor while ordering a pint at the bar in one of my locals. It was my first pint of the day.’

‘You get drunk that easy?’

‘No, I had just got through two bottles of cheap red wine in a Chinese restaurant. Alcohol normally just puts me to sleep.’

‘Christ Almighty!’ said Claire, pouring herself another glass. ‘What happened next?’

‘The poor young landlady ended up walking me home. It was slightly embarrassing going back in the pub the following day.’

‘You had to thank her I suppose.’

‘Exactly. And apologise.’

‘Look, here’s my business card. Would you be a darling and call me if you find Jonathan? I just want to know if the little bleeder is still alive and breathing, that’s all.’

‘You could easily go there and find out for yourself, couldn’t you?’

‘I could, but I won’t. I will never set foot on Portland again. Ever! Just one question before you go. Why are you so interested in finding him?’

‘It’s a long story. Sorry, my name’s Daniel. Here’s my number,’ I said, pulling my own card from my inside pocket.

‘I’m Claire.’

‘Ha, ha. Yes, I know. As I said, I’ve seen some of Jonathan’s paintings. They were hanging in the house of a murder victim close to where I live near Woking.’

‘What?’

‘It’s not a recent murder. As a matter of fact, the killing of Virna Babineaux happened over ten years ago. Would you have known her?’

‘No. Do you think Jonathan had something to do with it?’

‘Not directly. The killers were caught and eventually sentenced. It seems there may have been a possible romantic connection between Virna and Jonathan,’

‘Well, Jonathan could be romantic. He was a total ass as well. As soon as he got his little end away, his demeanour would change, and he’d immediately be out looking for the next unsuspecting woman. He could charm the hind legs off a donkey.’

‘Really?’

‘Yes, well. Nearly always. That’s if he didn’t get you pregnant.’

‘He didn’t, did he?’

‘No, but he got my friend Hilary’s twenty-seven-year-old daughter, Ella, pregnant. She lost it and ended up killing herself.’

‘Flipping heck, look, thanks for telling me all this. I must go now. Oh, I enjoyed the wine too. Thank you!’

‘Jonathan had a way of pissing everyone off, even without meaning to. I’ve never known anyone quite like him. Please remember to make that call if you do find anything. It’s important.’

‘I will. I promise.’

I suspected Claire still had feelings for Jonathan, despite all the name-calling. After grabbing fish and chips on the seafront, I caught the No.1 bus from Weymouth to Portland. Some twenty minutes later, I found myself in Fortunes Well, outside the Red Star Inn. It was now just gone two in the afternoon.

As I entered, the pub went quiet. It reminded me of that scene in the film, An American Werewolf in London when everything stops. The silence continued as I stepped up to the bar. The situation made me feel quite anxious.

‘Can I help?’

At least the young lady behind the bar was talking.

‘Oh, yes, a pint of Heineken, please.’

‘Oh, it’s off... Problem with the pump. We’ve got Peroni and Carlsberg.’

‘A pint of Peroni, please.’

‘£4.50 exactly.’

‘That’s cheap these days.’

‘Good, enjoy.’

I found myself a seat in the corner. The *Peroni* tasted quite tainted. A sign the pipes weren’t being cleaned properly. I thought it best not to say anything. I was now wondering how and who to ask about Jonathan. I wasn’t prepared to leave empty-handed and waste more of my time. A simple house number in Mallams would do. I couldn’t see anyone who could be Jonathan in the pub as if I would be lucky enough to meet him straight away.

‘Everything alright?’ asked the barmaid.

‘Err, yes,’ I said, lying through my teeth. ‘I would like a packet of crisps if you have any.’

‘Flavour? We have cheese and chive, prawn, salt and vinegar, and beef.’

‘I’ll go for the cheese and onion.’

‘I said it’s cheese and chives.’

‘Sorry, you did. A packet of those, please.’

I wasn’t sure if the barmaid was trying to be funny, plain awkward or if it was just her way. After a while, I noticed people were starting to whisper amongst themselves with the odd stare coming in my direction. A young guy went to a jukebox on the wall, pushing in some coins. Johnny Cash, Roy Orbison, and Hank Williams. The choice of songs somewhat surprised me, considering the guy’s young age. He then stepped behind the bar and took the lanyard from the girl who was serving. I noticed she was pouring herself a large glass of whiskey from an optic in front of the mirror. She stepped out and walked over to where I was sitting.

‘Mind if I sit here?’ she asked. ‘It’s the only seat left in the house.’

Her request surprised me as there were three sets of empty tables on the other side of the room—all vacant.

‘This is my usual seat. I always wait here for Daddy.’

‘I see you like the Jameson’s. That’s my favourite whiskey too.’

‘I prefer Southern Comfort, but John won’t bring it in anymore. He knows I’ll drink it. He caught me once and made me drink the rest of the bottle straight down in front of the whole pub. It made me very sick. I had a terrible hangover for days.’

‘You’re lucky he didn’t give you the sack.’

‘My daddy would have thumped him. He almost did when he found out John had made me drink the whole bottle down.’

‘I assume John is the landlord.’

‘Yes, he’s a dickhead. He likes to take all of his anger out on women, but Daddy is wise to him. He won’t get away with anything now.’

‘How long ago did all this happen?’

‘It was a long time ago. About fifteen years or so.’

‘Oh, I see. Is John also an artist?’

‘Ha, ha. Don't make me laugh. He can hardly write his own name. Talking about artists, we used to have an artist come here many years ago. He used to display his pictures on the wall. He sold quite a few.’

‘Was his name Jonathan?’

‘Yes.’

‘Jonathan Blackwell?’

‘Yes, do you know him?’

‘I know of him. Do you know what happened to him?’ I asked.

‘Fifteen years ago, when I was only about fourteen, he managed to get a woman pregnant. I was in here when it all went off. Her daddy came in and started throwing punches. Later, she lost the baby, and after about a year, she was found hanging from a tree up the road. They’ve since cut the tree down.’

‘I’ve heard he lives around the corner in Mallams.’

‘Not anymore. He left Fortunes Well about a week after the fight.’

‘When was that roughly, about 2007?’

‘I’d say more like 2006.’

‘Do you know where he went?’

‘Actually, I do. The artist owed John some money on the bar tab. He was always honest despite everything else. He wrote John a letter apologising for all the trouble he had caused. He had also enclosed a £20 postal order. There was a return address on the back of the envelope.’

‘Do you remember it?’

‘Isle of Wight. Freshwater, Isle of Wight. Please don’t ask me the rest, it was so long ago. I can’t remember.’

‘That’s a great help. Thank you. By the way, what’s your name?’

‘Rebecca.’

‘What’s the accent? I mean, where do you come from?’

‘I come from here. I come from Portland.’

Everyone in the pub looked up and laughed.

‘Have fun,’ she said. ‘I’ve got to go now. I can hear my daddy’s truck outside. Bye!’

‘Yeah, thanks, goodbye.’

Everything she said about Jonathan getting the girl pregnant ties in with the information Claire had given me. Weirdly as I left the pub, everyone gave me a smile and a cheery wave, with one of the women even saying, 'good luck.' They must have overheard the whole conversation after the music had stopped.

Now, to plan another excursion to the Isle of Wight. I was aware all this travelling was beginning to cost me time and money—quite a lot of money, which was outside my initial budget. I needed to start getting results, and quickly!

9

I hardly slept a wink last night, awoken by a tooting owl and the sound of barking foxes further down the Broadway. I sat up in bed, realising I was at a crossroads. I realised I had to focus. It occurred to me Virna's missing body and the empty house in Littlewick Road might not even be connected. It could all be a strange coincidence. Highly unlikely, though, and the more I thought about it, the more I convinced myself there had to be a connection.

Things got the better of me. It was about three o' clock. I opened the laptop, deciding my research needed to go further. How though? I was sure I had explored every angle already. The next thing I knew, daylight was sneaking through a crack in the curtains. I hadn't found or achieved anything.

I was about to shut the laptop down when I saw the name Bill Pattenden flash up on the screen. His name jumped out at me as he was my mentor at the Camberley Chronicle when I was younger. I remember him telling me once how to get to grips with a good story. How to dig deeper, never give up, and finally come up with a scoop. I opened his LinkedIn profile. He's a private consultant and publishing agent now. He must be getting on a bit. He was in his fifties when I knew him. I thought it would be a good idea to make contact and see if he fancied coming out for a drink, if only to talk about the good and bad old days at the Chronicle.

A quick phone call did the trick. Essentially, Bill remembered me. He always used to call me 'Blue Boy,' something to do with my surname and a pub where he used to drink over in Farnham. He agreed to meet me that same afternoon at his local, The Royal Standard, in Camberley.

'Wotcha, matey. Happy Saturday,' chortled a gruff voice as soon as I walked through the door.

'Hey Bill, how are you?'

'Bloody hell, where's all that weight come from? You were a skinny little runt the last time I saw you,' he said as he stood up and tried to give me a bear hug.

His trademark hug wasn't as tight as it used to be, but he still nearly winded me. Bill himself is still built like a brick shit-house. Apart from his greying hair and a strange choice of blue-framed spectacles, he hadn't changed. We worked out that the last time we saw each other was at Nancy Woolmer's funeral in 2004. Nancy was our former colleague at the Chronicle who died in a car crash on the M3 near Bagshot. She had just turned thirty-five.

'Such a sad loss, that young lady was. She was an excellent story-finder. Another one of my proteges I'll always be proud of,' said Bill trying to shield a crack in his voice.

'Yes, she was talented. A very pretty woman as well.'

'Indeed, she was. Extremely pretty,' Bill said, half raising his glass.

'And, is Binky Broomfield, the editor, still going? I always had the utmost respect for her.'

'Oh, Miss Brum! She retired a few years back and emigrated to Malta with her new husband, Geno. She died suddenly from a stroke a few months after arriving.'

'That is sad. Binky gave me my first newspaper job. I've always felt I owed her a lot.'

'I think we all did. She was one of the finest.'

'And what about Louise, Louise Burpham? Is she still at the Chronicle?'

'The receptionist? Oh no, they let her go about four or five years ago. Instant dismissal.'

'Flipping heck, what did she do?'

'She was always one to have a chip on her shoulder, usually about silly things. She was using the internet to set up fake social media accounts to harass people anonymously. Always tweeting about her work colleagues, malicious things, if you know what I mean.'

'That does surprise me!'

'Louise had a devilish mean streak and was very manipulative. Bob Glazier, who is the Chronicle's editor these days, had to discipline her numerous times. She was always cooking the books. I remember, in my time there, she was good at keeping a low profile. From what I gather, the police traced her to a computer she was using in the office.'

‘Oh, through the IP address.’

‘That’s it.’

‘Did they arrest her?’

‘Yes, she got off with a small fine and a community service order after pleading poverty. She was lucky!’

‘So, what’s she doing now?’

‘The last I heard, she was a cleaner in a pub somewhere, but telling everyone she was in fact the landlady.’

‘What, locally?’

‘I don’t know,’ said Bill as he waved at the barmaid.

‘It proves you never know some people. I always liked her, so that’s come as a total shock.’

‘There you go. Well, Blue Boy, what are you up to these days? I’ve heard you’ve left the Tribune.’

‘Yeah, I thought it was time to better myself and move on. The paper’s circulation had dropped, so there was no chance of a pay increase. Advertising revenue has also taken a knock. Morale is so bad over there now. I had to get out.’

‘And do what?’

‘I’ve set myself up as a freelance hack.’

‘Good luck with that. You are either very brave or just plain stupid.’

‘You’re not the first person to say that.’

‘How are you getting on with it?’

‘To use that predictable cliché, it’s certainly a learning curve. I thought I had done my homework, but obviously not. I rented some shared office space opposite Woking railway station. I’ve since realised it’s an expense I can ill-afford, so I cancelled the lease. Now, I am working from home.’

‘Very wise. The last thing you need is unnecessary overheads. Tell me, what’s your target audience? I mean, where are you going to sell your stories?’

‘I’ve got some bread-and-butter stuff to help pay the bills. Even supplying material to the Tribune, and its rival, the News & Mail. I’m also looking at the possibility of a couple of magazines and a national newspaper. They want to see some examples of my work. So, in some ways, it’s a catch-22 situation. My previous stuff from the Chronicle and the Tribune is all I have.’

‘No doubt they’ll tell you they will want to see something more recent.’

‘Exactly.’

‘Securing an income stream is the most difficult part of starting up on your own. Ideally, the stories should be looking for you.’

‘One is, although I’m a little worried I could be wasting my time.’

‘In my day, you could always smell a good story. Tell me…’

‘A friend of mine who’s in the police gave me details of a case. Her superiors had dropped it due to a lack of resources.’

‘Go on…’

‘I’ve been looking at it over the past few weeks. It goes back to the murder of a prostitute in London ten years ago. Now though, the story appears to have taken on two themes.’

‘How?’

‘Surrey Police were looking at a house in Knaphill that had been unlived in since the murder. Considering the property is supposedly vacant, the house has been well-maintained by a person or persons unknown. It should be decaying, derelict and overgrown by rights after ten years, but it’s not. A neighbour has said the only person she sees going in and out of the driveway is the postman. Mysteriously, the delivered post is always removed from the front porch.’

‘Are you telling me this house is haunted?’

‘I don’t think so. The neighbour, she’s a retired policewoman, by the way, let me in. I could smell furniture polish. The whole house is spotless.’

‘How’s the house connected to a murder?’

‘Its owner was the murder victim, a prostitute and former glamour model from France. Her name was Virna Babineaux.’

‘You said there are two themes. Was the murderer ever caught?’

‘Yes, Robert Surcouf and his accomplice, William Kuznia, were tried and sentenced around a year after it took place.’

‘Solved then?’

‘Yes, but there’s more. Virna Babineaux’s body had laid in West London Morgue since the murder. It was never claimed. A second autopsy was also recommended, but according to reports, it never took place. When I visited the morgue recently, I spoke to the senior pathologist, Juliet Edgar. She looked up some records and found vital mandatory drug analysis information was missing from the post-mortem examination in 2012.'

'Why wasn't a second autopsy carried out? Do you know?'

'According to Juliet, it was simply an oversight.'

'They could still do one now, couldn't they?'

'That's impossible.'

'Why?'

'After all those years, a cousin came over from France looking for Virna. Later, when the mortuary staff opened the unit where the body was stored, they noticed it was missing.'

'What?'

'My hunch is that it's something more sinister than just a simple oversight.'

'You mean, clerical error,' said Bill as he sipped his pint.

'Yes, I suppose so.'

'It certainly makes for a good story. Do you know any more?'

'There's a connection I'm still investigating. In the house in Knaphill, there are numerous paintings by an artist called Jonathan Blackwell. All the paintings have a message on the back signed by him and dedicated to Virna. I've already been to Weymouth and Portland in Dorset looking for him. That's when I found out he moved from there to the Isle of Wight some years ago. I intend to go over there quite soon and hopefully find him. It should be a good conversation.'

'And one you hope will tie up your story?'

'I hope so.'

'Don't bank on it. This artist bloke probably has nothing to do with the missing body. All you'll get from him is his reminiscence of the French lady from his past. He might not even want to talk about her. It will be a particularly sore point if he knows she's dead, which he probably does. I wouldn't want someone sniffing around asking questions after all this time.'

'So, what should I do?'

'You said the police case was closed?'

'I did.'

'Listen, Surrey Police may have shut up on the house in Knaphill, but what about the Met?'

'What about them?'

'If a body's gone missing from a morgue on their patch, mark my word, there's no chance they will close the case. That will stay open until the mystery is solved.'

'My friend Sue was adamant the case was closed.'

'Yes, but she's probably only talking from the Surrey Police perspective. You need to check this all out, otherwise, you could find yourself in hot water. Someone in the Metropolitan Police could even identify you as a potential suspect.'

'I can't see how.'

'Simply by asking questions. To them, you will quickly become a person of interest. My advice would be to contact them now and tell them who you are, why you're interested in the case and who gave you all your initial information. You will still need to be very careful. In my experience, unless you can reveal your leads and provide them with some hard evidence, they won't like you sticking your nose in.'

'I see. Thanks for the warning. Now, can you understand why I needed to speak with you?'

'Yes, but you need to get the basics right. It seems you've gone into everything like a bull in a china shop. You need to step back and take a break. I'd say give it a few days. When you return to your desk or computer or whatever you have, start a timeline of events and keep track of where you are. You should always cover yourself!'

'Good advice, I will, thanks.'

'It's common sense, that's all.'

It was good to see Bill was still his usual self after all these years. He's very assertive with what he says and can sometimes be intimidating. That said, he has a knack for asking questions from a different perspective, for which I've always admired him. While Bill was in the loo, the barmaid finally brought over some more drinks.

'Since when has Blue Boy been drinking whiskey?' Bill asked.

'A few years on and off. I see you're still a real ale man.'

'Love the stuff. You rarely get a bad pint in here. I still like a good glass of red wine, mind.'

'Yes, I remember your wine rack at the Chronicle.'

‘Those were the days,’ said Bill, raising his glass. ‘Now listen, I’ve been thinking about this story you’ve just been telling me about. Do you need some help?’

‘Our conversation just now has already been a great help. Thank you!’

‘I mean practical help. Someone who can do some of the footwork for you.’

‘I think I’ll be okay. Anyway, I haven’t got the finances to pay for any extra help. That’s why I’ve decided to give up the office space and work from home already.’

‘Listen. I have a young lady who sometimes works for me. She’s at a loose end at present. She could do with some more reporting experience. I was looking for someone who could help her with that anyway. She’s on my books, so you won’t have to worry about money.’

‘Young lady?’

‘I thought that would make your ears prick up. It is just your ears, isn’t it?’

I laughed. ‘Yes, I think so. Thank you very much for the offer. What’s her name?’

‘Anouska, but she calls herself Annie.’

‘Is that Russian?’

‘Ukrainian.’

‘That’s fortunate!’

‘Don’t forget. Many Russians are also victims of Mr Putin’s war.’

‘Yeah, good point.’

‘Listen, here’s her card. Call her. I’ll let her know you might be in touch.’

‘Thank you.’

I wasn’t sure if I needed any more help. Not knowing how my story was going to unfold, it wasn't easy to make any sort of commitment.

‘It’s been good to see you, Blue Boy.’

‘Good to see you too, Bill, and thanks again.’

‘Remember what I said about the basics!’

‘I will, I promise.’

‘Let me know how you get on. Once you’ve got your story, come to me first.’

‘Oh, you want your ten per cent,’ I said, laughing.

‘Too right. This is where my expertise will be of use to you. If you write your story well, you’re talking about at least four figures. Five if it's sensational-soaraway-Sun stuff!’

Bill’s last comment put me in a slight dilemma. Morale code and all that. I agree with sticking to the basics and writing a good, robust, sensitive story. Let’s put it this way, I’m not really a fan of red-top journalism.

10

To be honest, I had already shelved the idea of contacting Annie, as Bill had suggested, but she didn't take too long to contact me. She seemed quite pushy on the phone and was already asking many questions. Her voice had an intriguing dominance and a persuasive ring to it, which, against my will, somehow won me over.

We arranged to meet in London at the Caffe Nero on the Southbank by the Oxo Tower. More expense, I thought! Apparently, Annie lives in Kennington and works from home almost permanently. She told me she visits Bill on the first Monday of each month for a catch-up and regular debrief. She had been down to Camberley to see him yesterday, hence her quick response after I saw Bill on Saturday.

I arrived at Nero's slightly early. It was ten o'clock, and the place was beginning to fill quite quickly. I could see what Annie looked like from her WhatsApp image. So, I knew who to look out for. She had already seen my LinkedIn profile, so recognising each other wasn't a problem.

'You must be Daniel,' said a voice behind me as I took a sip of my black Americano.

'I am indeed. You must be Annie.'

'I am.'

'Okay. Would you like a coffee?'

'Of course, I'll have a small cappuccino, please.'

'Coming up.'

'I'm so pleased to meet you. Bill has told me a lot about you. He said you used to work together at the Camberley Chronicle,' she said excitedly.

'That's right. Bill taught me quite a lot. He's what you might call the last of the old-school journalists. I've always had a lot of respect for him. He was a great mentor.'

'I understand that. He still is. I love him. Bill's a great man. He treats me well and is always spoiling me.'

'In what sense? Not like a sugar daddy, I hope.'

'He provides me with work. What else were you thinking?'

'Nothing. I was just wondering what you were going to say next.'

'Ha, ha. I think even Bill knows when to stop. Anyway, it appears you're working on a terrific story. From what Bill said, it sounds like a lively one. He said I should be able to help you with all the basics. Does that ring any bells?'

'Typical Bill,' I said, raising my eyebrows.

'How did Bill get involved?'

'It all happened quite fast. I was wondering which direction to take as I had come to a junction with the story. Bill's name flashed up in my LinkedIn account, I called him out of the blue for some advice, and the next thing I knew, we were sitting in the Royal Standard the same afternoon reminiscing about the old days.'

'Bill was so excited by what you told him. He thinks you're onto something unique. That's why I'm here to help. I've already done a little research. It's all about a lady called Virna Babineaux, isn't it?'

'Yes. I must say, you haven't wasted any time.'

'I don't intend to. I like to get my teeth into things and see them through to completion. Bill said I must help you!'

'Did he now?' I said with a wry smile.

'It's a little noisy in here, my lovely. We might have to find somewhere quieter, so we can talk. I know a little oasis not too far away. Come on, let's go.'

Annie looks in her mid to late twenties. She came over as quite abrupt at first. She's undoubtedly assertive and very confident. I got the impression she wouldn't take the word 'no' for an answer. She was also very pretty, with long curly red hair and deep green eyes. Somehow it was her eyebrows that drew me in. I noticed a small tattoo of a scorpion on the inside of her right wrist. It didn't seem to match her personality. 'It's a defiant mark of one's identity,' she said when she saw me looking.

Annie suggested going around the corner to a little seated area called Bernie Spain gardens.

'It's in the middle of the city, but somehow, I always find it peaceful here,' she said as we arrived. 'It feels like a little piece of the countryside.'

'Yeah, it's nice. I see what you mean. It's quite surprising what you find in London when you look around.'

'The gardens are named after a local activist, Bernadette Spain, who served the local Coin Street community. She died while still quite young in 1984. Such a shame,' said Annie. 'It's one of my favourite places. We should now be able to hear ourselves think,' she added.

'Good! So, how do you think you can help?' I asked.

'As I said. I've done a little research already. I know about the murder, and Bill told me about the mystery surrounding the house near where you live.'

'I'm glad he's filled you in.'

'I saw some of the newspaper reports online. I'm sure they're the same ones you've been looking at.'

'I'm sure they are. Have you managed to find anything new?'

'Yes, I've discovered a famous French photographer. Her name is Ros Muller.'

'Yes, her name came up when I was doing a search.'

'Did you see Virna was one of her models?

'Yes, that's how I found all the photographs of Virna.'

'It appears Ros Muller published her memoirs in 2017 and frequently mentioned your lady, Virna. She explains how upset she felt when she heard Virna was killed in London. According to what Ms Muller has written, they even had a lesbian fling while Virna was at the peak of her modelling career.'

'Flipping heck, I'm impressed.'

'Ms Muller talks about how Virna was influenced by a guy called Robert Surcouf. She blames him for wrecking Virna's career and says it was no surprise when she found out that it was him who killed her.'

'This is all good stuff.'

'I'll zap you the link to the article. One thing that will interest you is this,' said Annie showing me the article on her phone. 'Look, see what Ms Muller says here. "Virna has no family, not that I know of anyway. I formally requested to bring her back to Paris for a proper burial, but the authorities won't allow her body's release from the morgue because I am not family." Impressed?'

‘That’s incredible. That may explain why the body was kept so long.’

‘It may also explain why it has gone missing,’ said Annie quite smugly.

‘You’re right. Ros Muller could be behind its disappearance. All this has to be worth following up. One problem, though. Ros Muller died in 2019.’

‘Yes, I saw that. So, maybe she wasn’t responsible?’

‘I’ve also discovered that Ros was living with a woman called Luisella Cabane. We could go to Paris and speak to Ms Cabane. She may remember something!’

‘What?’

‘I also found her full address. The article states that she lives in Avenue du Bois, Antony, a suburban town on the outskirts of Paris. With that, I did another search and found her house number. BINGO!’

‘Do you get these results when you work for Bill?’

‘Most of the time. Sometimes it’s down to hard graft. Other times, it’s just pure luck.’

‘Now I know why he rates you so highly.’

Annie laughed. ‘Thank you. I didn’t know that.’

‘You mean he’s never told you?’

‘No, not really.’

‘More fool him. I’m sure he must be smitten with you.’

‘Smitten, no. Bill is aware of the boundaries, and I respect him for that. Now, changing the subject, what about you? Are you married?’

‘No, I’ve managed to swerve that. I couldn’t marry the person I wanted to, so I’ve never been interested in anyone else.’

‘No-one?’

‘Not at all.’

‘I’m sure you could find someone if you wanted to. There are lots of women available on the internet. You only have to look at the dating sites.’

‘No, not my thing. I was in love once, and it broke me when it all went pear-shaped. There’s no way I can go down that road again.’

‘What happened?’

‘She was a lot younger than me.’

‘Age shouldn’t be a barrier. It’s just a number.’

‘I know, but in a round-about way, it was. Leanna decided to return to university and get her master’s degree as a mature student. It’s what she wanted. She was a keen archaeologist, fanatical. She wanted all the letters after her name. When she got them, she became a different person. She just wasn’t my Leanna anymore. Things weren’t the same. In the end, we drifted apart. She moved to Canada and became a professor. Now, she’s quite famous over there giving television lectures to students.’

‘And you’ve never been interested in anyone else?’

‘I’m always interested. I just don’t want to fall in love again. I was seeing someone called Sue until recently. That fell by the wayside after about a year.’

‘They say love hurts.’

‘Love? Ha, ha. I’m sure it does!’

‘Are you off women now altogether? No, sorry, I’m getting carried away. Don’t answer that.’

‘Yeah, you were getting a little too personal,’ I laughed.

‘Sorry. I like talking about these things. It helps me get to know people better.’

‘Is that a Ukrainian thing?’

‘I don’t know. I’m from Russia.’

‘Bill told me you were Ukrainian!’

‘I think he’s trying to protect me because of all this war nonsense. I’ve lived here in England since I was three, so it shouldn’t make any difference.’

‘I wondered why I didn’t detect too much of an accent. Are your parents here?’

‘No, they both died when I was little. I went to live with my older sister and her English husband, Christopher. They brought me up as their own.’

‘Where are they now?’

‘Unfortunately, they separated a few years ago when I was at university in Leeds. Svetlana went back to Russia. I still see my adoptive dad. He lives in Cornwall now and has a lovely cottage overlooking the sea. I go down and see him sometimes.’

‘Adoptive dad?’

‘Yes, Christopher and Svetlana, adopted me. It was easier for them if I had the same surname rather than explaining away my

Russian name and the death of my parents all the time. That's why I'm now known as Annie Parsons.'

'Bill said your real name is Anouska?'

'On paper, yes, that's my name, but I prefer Annie. Everyone calls me Annie these days.'

'Except Bill, of course.'

'Yeah, sometimes. He likes calling me by my full name. "It's such a beautiful name. Why shorten it?" he keeps saying. Do people call you Dan or Danny?'

'Sometimes, but I hate it. I always prefer Daniel. After all, that's what my parents named me. It's a Jewish thing and all about respect. If someone tries to shorten my name, it makes me angry.'

'You don't look Jewish.'

'Good, I don't consider myself to be of any religion. I'm an atheist. I don't believe in God.'

'Really?'

'Yes, really. My grandpop, Lionel, was a rabbi in his day. He died a few months after I was born.'

'With you being an atheist, the poor man must be turning over in his grave.'

'Probably, we all have our cross to bear.'

'That's a contradiction in terms.'

'What is?'

'You just told me you're an atheist.'

'Oh, ah, yes. I see what you mean.'

We both laughed.

'So, what about you, are you married,' I asked.

'No.'

'Boyfriend?'

'No, the bastard dumped me by text.'

'Why?'

'Do you mind if I hold back on that. I'll tell you another time. I promise.'

'Oh, okay. Sorry. I didn't mean to upset you.'

'Don't worry, you haven't. It's me. I'm being silly, that's all.'

'So long as that's all it is.'

'It seems we both have interesting backgrounds,' said Annie looking at her watch. 'Look, my lovely, time is getting short. I need to get across to Hampstead for another meeting.'

'Oh, okay.'

'Look, I'll zap you that link, I promise. I'll do some more research when I get back this evening. Next time we meet, we can talk about Paris if you're up to it?'

'Yes, I'm up for it,' I said hesitantly, as Annie waved goodbye.

On the train home, I couldn't help wondering what I was getting myself into.

11

A week on, Annie still hadn't sent the link over to me as promised. Fortunately, I found the article myself, along with a couple of others.

Regarding Paris, I couldn't see any real benefit in making a trip to speak to someone who may not know anything or, if they did, probably wouldn't want to talk about it anyway. That problem solved itself when I found an online obituary for Luisella Cabane. She died back in February this year.

The notorious French porn actress and former glamour model Luisella Cabane has died suddenly in Paris, aged 52. The star passed away peacefully after a short illness at 10.00 local time (0900 GMT) on Sunday, her daughter, Daphne Cabane told Le Figaro.

'The queen of the twilight screen has left us all to make another star, Luisella's confidante, Jed Dombrowski, said in a statement on behalf of the late star's close family.

Cabane gained fame as one of Ros Muller, the acclaimed photographer's subjects in the award-winning collection, 'Basque Heroines' and after appearing in the controversial, 'Le dernier des héros rampants' (The Last of the Rampant Heroes)' a film based on the sordid sex life of an 'unnamed' French president, produced by Stefan La Fort.

Realising I was spending too much time looking at the computer, I decided to act positively and move on with a trip to the Isle of Wight. I've traced Jonathan Blackwell's full address, which shows that he was living at 1 El Alamein Mews, Freshwater, three years ago.

I took the train from Woking to Lymington, changing at Brockenhurst. Then, it was a pleasant thirty-minute trip on a ferry called the 'Wight Sun' to Yarmouth and then a No.7 bus to Freshwater.

On arrival, I could see that there wasn't much open. My first intended port of call was an art gallery called Heaney's, but according to a sign in the window, it was closed until next Spring. This was frustrating as I saw one of Jonathan's paintings on a back wall. It was of a woman with darkened eyes at a car's steering wheel, like one I had seen in Virna's house in Knaphill.

I paced up and down outside the shop a couple of times, looking at the map on my phone to see how far I was from his address.

'Can I help you?'

I looked up and saw a guy about my age looking down from a window above the shop.

'I hope so!'

'Wait there. I'll come down.'

After about five minutes, he appeared at the shop's front door. His hair was pulled back in a ponytail, and he was wearing a pink sweatshirt and light blue dungarees.

'What are you looking for?' he asked. 'We're closed.'

'Yes, yes, I can see that. I've come over from Surrey. I'm a journalist, and I'm working on a story which involves an artist.'

'Which one?'

'Jonathan Blackwell. Do you know him?'

'I used to. I haven't seen him for a couple of years. We have one of his paintings for sale.'

'Yes, I could see it through the window.'

'Do you want to buy it?'

'How much?'

'£1,250.'

'Flipping heck, that's, err, pricey.'

'Take it or leave it.'

'I'll take a rain check on that one,' I said.

'Most people do,' he laughed, 'though we sell quite a lot of work in and around that price range.'

'Thanks.'

'What interests you in Blackwell?'

'I'm working on a story. A woman was murdered in London ten years ago. Her house in Surrey still has several of his paintings on the wall. I've also found personal references from Jonathan to the victim, perhaps romantically connecting the two.'

'Romantic? We used to call him the last Bohemian around here. He had a very cavalier attitude. It was almost like he had been transported from another age. He was very odd. All the women liked him, though.'

'And you say you haven't seen him for a couple of years. Do you know why?'

'Mm, I do know Blackwell was married to the woman from the church, the flower arranger. I don't know much more than that, although I did hear there was some sort of ruck between them.'

'What age would you say Jonathan was?'

'Easily in his late seventies. I'd say seventy-seven, seventy-eight, something like that.'

'What does he look like?'

'Like most old men. Stooped, bald as a coot, you know. He was always quite lively though, and he always had a harem of women in tow.'

'Not like this then,' I said, showing the guy the *Southern Evening Echo* photo from 2001 which I had downloaded on my phone.'

'Mm, I remember him saying once that he had long hair. Yeah, that's him, alright.'

'And what about his wife?'

'She must be younger. A lot younger. I'd put her around fifty-something.'

'Right, okay. Thank you. You've been very helpful.'

'Do you want his address? I believe I still have it on file.'

'If it's 1, El Alamein Mews, then I have it.'

'That sounds about right. Good luck. Who do you write for anyway?'

'I'm freelance.'

'Oh. Oh well, good luck anyway.'

'Thanks.'

People always give that reaction when I say I'm a freelance journalist. It's as if they think I'm some poor imitation of Walter Mitty, wandering around pretending to be a reporter rather than being employed by an actual newspaper. I've already seen the difference in attitudes since I left the Tribune. Some people are so fickle!

When I reached El Alamein Mews, I noticed all the house numbers were odd. No even numbers as such. I walked up the gravel drive to No.1. An old yellow Volkswagen camper van was rusting away at the side. I noticed a curtain twitch in the window directly above the porch. I pushed the button to ring the doorbell and waited. There was no answer. I rang the bell again. Nothing. After two minutes, I stepped back and looked at the house again. This time I saw a name plaque next to the porch. The place was called 'Potential'. If nothing else, I knew I could easily remember it.

After leaving my card at the door, I chose to leave immediately. The discovery had a strange effect on me, and after a week with no alcohol, I knew I needed a drink!

I found a pub called The Vyne, which had only just opened for the day. The weather was surprisingly warm for October, so I sat outside in the beer garden with a pint of the local bitter. I had purposely left the whiskey alone, knowing that one would probably lead to two, three or maybe even four. I had been trying my hardest to do what the doctor ordered, but life was getting in the way. I knew I would have to try and move in different circles.

I became mesmerised by a family of red squirrels running up and down the lawn, jumping onto a pub table and inspecting some peanuts someone had left. I don't think they liked the salt. As I stood, they all ran off and disappeared up a nearby maple tree.

The next thing I knew, I was back inside the pub, ordering myself a second pint. Something I had promised myself I wouldn't do. It was more habitual than intentional, and that was worrying.

'You look as if you have the weight of the world on your shoulders,' said the woman behind the bar as she pressed the change into my hand.

'You can say that again,' I said, looking around for a seat inside.

'I'm Kathy, by the way.'

'You sound Irish.'

'That I am. I came over from Donegal in 1982. Been here ever since.'

'Have you never thought about going back?'

‘I did think about it once. My family is here now. I have three daughters and a grandchild to think about. This pub is their home, and I need to be here for them.’

‘Do you have a husband?’

‘Oh yes, Harry, he’s quite ancient, you know. He struggles and is unsteady on his feet, but he still manages a couple of rounds on the golf course each week.’

‘Good for him.’

‘If you don’t mind me saying, I don’t think I’ve seen you in here before.’

‘You haven’t. Sorry, my name’s Daniel, by the way.’

‘I’m pleased to meet you, Daniel, so I am.’

‘I was wondering. You say you’ve been here since the 1980s. Have you ever come across an artist called Jonathan Blackwell?’

‘Old, Jonnie, of course. He used to be a permanent fixture in here. That was his usual seat over there,’ Kathy said, pointing to an armchair in the corner. ‘We still call it “Jonnie’s chair”, even now.’

‘I spoke to the guy who owns Heaney’*s* art gallery earlier. He said he hadn’t seen Jonathan for a couple of years. He still has one of his paintings on display.’

‘We have one too,’ said Kathy, inviting me through to the other bar. ‘It’s a portrait.’

‘Who of?’

‘That’s my eldest daughter Siobhan. She was about thirty-years old when she posed for that.’

‘Now you’re giving your age away,’ I said with a chuckle.

‘I’m sixty-one, so I am.’

‘You don’t look it if you don’t mind me saying so.’

‘You, flatterer, you. You can come again.’

I laughed. ‘Thank you.’

‘Okay, tell me, Daniel. Why are you asking about Jonnie?’

‘It’s a long story. I’ve just been round to his home in El Alamein Mews. There was no answer, but I’m sure someone was in there.’

‘That would have been Jilly.’

‘Jilly?’

‘Yes, his wife. Jonnie left her for a French woman he said he met down at the Bay Café. At the end of 2019, I think it was.’

'Flipping heck.'

'Do you know her name?'

'That I don't. It all happened very quickly. I know Jonnie and Jilly were frequently arguing towards the end. People often came here and told me they had seen a police car outside their house. After he left, there was an auction of all his paintings. He used to keep them in the back of a camper van.'

'I've seen it on the driveway.'

'Yes, it's still there. Jonnie loved driving that thing around. We held the auction here and made a fortune for charity. Jilly didn't want a penny of it. His paintings are still what you might call trendy, I believe.'

'Yes, I know.'

'Come on. Tell me what's happened. Are you the police?'

'No, I'm just a news reporter working on a story.'

'That's a relief. Why are you so interested in Jonnie, though?'

'Ten years ago, a French woman called Virna Babineaux was murdered in London. Quite a few of Jonathan's paintings were found in her house near where I live and work in Surrey. On the back of each painting is a personal message from Jonathan to Virna.'

'He didn't kill her, did he?'

'No, definitely not. The suspects were caught and brought to justice. I only want to ask Jonathan some questions about Virna.'

'Oh, I see. It all sounds very tragic, so it does.'

'Do you think Jilly will know anything?'

'She won't talk to you. She doesn't talk to anyone anymore. Since the auction, she's kept herself tucked away in that house like a recluse. When she does venture out, it seems like she's frightened of her own shadow. I tried to approach her once outside the Memorial Hall up the road, but she ran inside and told me to leave her alone. Other people have had similar experiences with her, so they have.'

'It sounds like she needs help.'

'That's what everyone has been saying, but she's not helping herself.'

'Are you telling me it's not worth going back and trying her door again?'

'That I am. You'll be wasting your time.'

'Oh, okay, thanks.'
'Would you like another drink, Daniel?'
'Oh, yes, a large Jameson's, please.'
'Coming up.'

12

I was still disappointed that I had given in to the alcohol so easily on the Isle of Wight. I realised it was more difficult to shake the habit than I thought. I knew things couldn't go on like this. Amongst others, Sue said I should seek counselling, but then I didn't want to admit I had a problem. She suggested I could be an alcoholic. 'No, no, no,' I said. She wasn't the first to say I was in denial. Just as I was ripping myself apart with all the brutal self-analysis, I received an unexpected call from Iona Turner.

'Daniel, dear. Is that you? It's Iona.'

'Hello. How are you? Good to hear from you. Is everything alright?'

'Oh, yes. I'm fine. I'm calling about the house next door.'

'Why? What's happened?'

'When did you come and see me? It must have been a few weeks ago.'

'It was. Hang on. I'll have the date here somewhere. Oh yes, Tuesday 20 September. Why?'

'Since you visited, no-one has changed the flowers in the window. I sneaked in there yesterday, and nothing has been cleaned. Cobwebs are beginning to appear everywhere.'

'Do you think my visit may have frightened them off?'

'Them? I'm not sure. It's all quite bizarre. It's the first time this has happened in all these years.'

'Since Virna died?'

'Ms Babineaux? Yes!'

'Do you think it could be a coincidence?'

'I'm not sure. I don't think so.'

'Why?'

'Perhaps something has happened to the person who was going in there. Perhaps they've died or something.'

'Is there something you're not telling me?'

'No, I've told you everything. As I said, no-one has been there since you came to see me that day.'

'It's all very odd. Would you like me to come round?'

'No, dear. There's no need for that.'

'Okay, but you will tell me if anything changes, won't you?'

'Of course. I'll keep a close watch and let you know.'

'As soon as it happens?'

'Yes, dear, I promise.'

Not having spoken to Iona on the phone before, I wasn't sure how she sounded. She didn't sound agitated, upset or anything. Indeed, she came over as very matter-of-fact.

Soon after, another call came, this time from Annie.

'Hi Daniel, my lovely. Sorry it's taken me a while to get in touch. I've only just realised I forgot to zap that link over.'

'Don't worry. I found the article myself.'

'What do you think?'

'I think Paris is off. I found an obituary for someone called Luisella Cabane.'

'Yes, I saw that the other day. That's one of the things I wanted to talk to you about.'

'If she's dead, there's no-one left in France to talk to.'

'Oh, yes, there is. The basics, Daniel. The basics.'

'What do you mean?'

'Have you got your laptop open?'

'Yes.'

'Go back to the article.'

'What, the obituary?'

'Yes.'

'Hang on, oh, right. Here it is. What about it?'

'Read me the first four lines.'

'The notorious French porn actress and former glamour model, Luisella Cabane, has died suddenly in Paris, aged 52. The star passed away peacefully after a short illness at 10.00 local time (0900 GMT) on Sunday, her daughter, Daphne Cabane, told Le Figaro.

'Do you see it?' she asked.

'What?'

'The obvious. I'm talking about the basics. Remember what Bill was telling you about the basics.'

'Sorry, I still don't see it.'

'Then, sorry back, my lovely, you must be fucking blind!'

'Maybe I am!'

'Daphne Cabane!'

'Oh, the daughter, yes. What about her?'

'For fuck's sake, Daniel. Don't you see it? We can go and speak to her. Think about all the things she might know!'

'I didn't think of that.'

'Of course you didn't.'

'So, what next?'

'In a few days, we'll go to St Pancras and catch a train to Paris.'

'What? So, who's paying?'

'Don't worry about that. It's sorted. I've spoken to Bill. He said he'll pay. I'll put it down on my expenses.'

'Expenses?'

'Yes, well, I am employed by him, aren't I?'

'Bill's consultancy must be doing well if he can afford to pay for people to visit France.'

'That's nothing. Last year he sent me to New York. We were covering a fraud case. All I had to do was go there and pinpoint where the main suspect lived. Don't tell Bill, but I'd already looked it up on the internet before I flew out.'

'A bit ironic as you were working on a fraud case then.' I said, chuckling.

'Don't be like that. I considered it a perk. A free transatlantic break if you will. Anyway, Bill gets his rewards in other ways.'

'What other ways?'

'Ha, ha. That would be telling, my lovely.'

'I thought you said you don't let Bill too close. I remember you saying that you keep him at arm's length.'

'That I do, I most certainly do.'

'I'm confused.'

'You should be. I will demonstrate exactly what I mean when the time is right.'

After Annie's call, I couldn't stop thinking about what she meant. I was also embarrassed that I didn't pick up on Daphne Cabane. That could be an essential connection, and Bill was right. I do need to brush up on the basics!

Still not knowing who Annie or Anouska really was. I decided to do a quick Google search on her. At first, nothing. I then remembered something she said about going to university in Leeds. She also briefly mentioned a mentor's importance in helping her gain academic recognition for some of her early papers.

Eventually, I traced a couple of articles she had written for an online magazine called The Gryphon. Interestingly one of these covered the closure of a brothel owned by a woman whose exploits had been featured on TV in 2012. After following a couple of links, I realised that Annie was interested in writing about prostitution and BDSM. She had also been interviewed by the Yorkshire Evening Post.

Annie was writing and talking openly about sex and her own experiences, even advocating the legalisation of brothels.

I decided to explore a BDSM website which was based in Leeds. It was a directory of local women offering their S&M services but hadn't been updated since 2017. I decided to keep looking through, and then came the shock…

I'm Alice, based in a lovely luxury apartment ten minutes from Leeds train station. We have use of my fully equipped playroom and parlour and kinky mirrored boudoir. On arrival, protocol will be established to ensure discretion for us both. Shower facilities, toiletries and clean towels are provided. I will expect you to be clean and smelling nice for me.

I am a discerning lady who picks her playthings carefully. I know what I enjoy, and I like to tease mercilessly. Please follow the link below if you want to contact me. I want to get to know you a little before we meet.

It wasn't so much the message that caught my eye. It was a series of photographs: a black and red leather corset, fishnet stockings, and black leather boots. The model's face was blurred out, but something was very familiar—a black scorpion tattoo on the inside of her right wrist. I zoomed in. I could then convince myself that these pictures were of Annie, albeit taken some five years ago. Now, things were starting to make sense. Anouska, Annie and now Alice. All the same person. What she said about Bill, the cryptic innuendos, became quite clear. Annie as a reporter had good reason to be interested in my case. Do I tell her

I've found out about her past? Or do I go with the flow? Ironically, it was Bill who once said to me that only dead fish do that!

My next conversation with Annie was going to be an interesting one.

13

There wasn't to be a 'next' conversation with Annie. Curiously, all communication with her had stopped. Two weeks had passed since she was last in contact. This seemed to be all the stranger as it happened so soon after I discovered what she was up to whilst at university. There's no way she could have known I'd found her web page unless I were missing something obvious.

I decided to contact Bill to see if he knew anything, so I made the call.

'Hi Bill, it's Daniel.'

'Blue Boy, I was wondering when I would hear from you. Did you get my email?'

'Err, no.'

'Have you checked?'

'Hold on. I'm just going through the recent ones on my phone now.'

'I sent it about a week ago. Have you looked in your spam box?'

'Just looking. Oh yeah. Found it.'

'You need to change your filter by the sound of it.'

'So, you've pulled Annie off my case.'

'Yes. I had no option.'

'Why?'

'It's personal. She had said a couple of things about me which reached the wrong people, including my wife.'

'Oh, I see!' I said, wondering if I should say any more.

'It's all history now. I had to save myself from any further embarrassment. I paid the young lady up to the end of next month and let her go.'

'That's a shame. She was proving quite useful.'

'I'm sure she was. Hopefully, I've saved you from a fate worse than death.'

'Ha, ha. I'm not sure what you mean.'

'Let's leave it there. How are you getting on with your story anyway?'

'To be honest, it's come to something of a standstill. Nothing has happened recently, except whoever went into Virna Babineaux's old house in Knaphill has apparently stopped visiting.'

'How do you know?'

'The neighbour, Iona Turner, phoned me. She had noticed the flowers hadn't been changed in the window. She said she'd been to the house and had a good look around. Nothing had been cleaned, and there were cobwebs everywhere.'

'Interesting.'

'Also, I was trying to follow up on a couple of leads in Paris. One was Luisella Cabane, but I saw she had died. Annie suggested that we could go and speak to her daughter, Daphne. That was the last time I spoke to her.'

'Yes. She did tell me.'

'And you were going to pay for us to catch a train to Paris!'

'Excuse me? I don't think so. I'm not made of money.'

'Oops, sorry. Annie inferred that you were.'

'I think she had the wrong impression of me. I'm not an easy touch and certainly not one to be blackmailed.'

'Blackmailed?'

'Look, just carry on with what you're doing. If you need any further help, call, or email me. I wish I hadn't set Annie loose on you now, but I wasn't to know what was about to happen. I'll leave that all to your imagination. Can I trust you?'

'Yes, of course.'

'Good man. And remember what I told you.'

'What? Stick to the basics?'

'You got it in one!'

Bill seemed quite upbeat on the phone, but I sensed his voice was hiding something. I wondered if Annie's extra-curricular activities had caused a problem. I kept thinking his decision to get rid of her may have done me a favour. However, towards the end, I was beginning to quite like her.

The next thing I knew, there was a BANG, BANG, BANG on my front door. I was only wearing my boxer shorts, so I hurriedly threw on my dressing gown and went through the hallway to answer.

'Living the life of Riley, now, are we?'

‘Fucking hell!’ It was Sue.

‘Hi Hun, can I come in? I’ve got some news for you.’

‘What news?’

‘Put the kettle on, and I’ll tell you.’

‘What then?’

‘It’s about Iona Turner. She’s in ICU.’

‘What?’

‘She’s in the intensive care unit in Frimley Park Hospital. It’s not looking good.’

‘Well, she is an old lady.’

‘No, no, it’s nothing like that. Sixty-seven is not that old! We had a call yesterday. A neighbour living on the other side of Virna Babineaux’s old property heard a commotion and some screams. He rushed round and found Iona lying face down in Babineaux’s old garden. My colleague, DC Craig Dunlop, was able to revive her as I called for backup and chased up the ambulance.’

‘Flipping heck!’

‘Are you still looking into the story?’

‘Yes.’

‘I suggest you back off until all this blows over.’

‘Are you telling me the cold case has become hot again?’

‘No, definitely not. It’s a new case altogether. We’re not even fully sure if there’s a connection between Iona’s attack and all the other strange shenanigans. When was the last time you saw Iona anyway?’

‘That was way back in September, shortly after you gave me the heads up about a possible story. She did call me recently though.’

‘What about?’

‘About the flowers not being changed in the window. About the house no longer being cleaned. She seemed most perturbed and was telling me about all the cobwebs.’

‘Yes, we noticed the flowers in the vase were dead.’

‘Poor Iona. Do you know who might have attacked her?’

‘The forensic team have gathered some fingerprints and DNA. Now, are you going to pour me this tea or what?’

‘Sorry, there you go.’

‘Thanks. Forensics found blood on a concrete slab in the garden. The samples contain what we believe are the attacker’s

DNA. There's something not quite right, so it's undergoing further analysis.'

'That concrete slab covers an old well, doesn't it? I tried to open it up when I went round there that day with Iona, but I couldn't budge it.'

'The cover was partially removed when we arrived. Craig and Mr Peters, the neighbour who called it in, pulled it fully open once we had the heads up from Forensics.'

'That well must be quite deep.'

'It's not actually a well. It's the entrance to a tunnel.'

'What?'

'The tunnel goes off in two directions. Northward for about 100 metres until it comes to a sudden stop and south into the basement of the house. This is where we believe the intruder has been gaining entry all these years.'

'Fucking hell. I didn't know the house had a basement.'

'It's a small cellar. Craig and a couple of uniformed officers went down there. Apart from copious amounts of wine, they found a fold-up bed, a small refrigerator, some BDSM magazines and a French newspaper.'

'French newspaper?'

'Yes, dated Tuesday, 20th September.'

'Shit, that's the same day I visited Iona.'

'*La Figaro*,' said Sue, reaching to show me a picture on her phone.

'That's the very same paper I found online, which has been reporting on the people Virna used to be connected with. Her photographer, Ros Muller, and Muller's lesbian companion, Luisella Cabane. Did you know they are both dead now?'

'Yes, Daniel, I know. We've done the homework.'

'I was going to speak with Ms Cabane's daughter, Daphne, next.'

'DON'T' shouted Sue abruptly. 'Leave it alone for now. Our contacts at Europol are already on to her. If I hear anything, I'll let you know if I can.'

'Does this now mean that I've been wasting my time?'

'Not necessarily. You can still find out what happened to Babineaux's body, but please keep a low profile. I don't need you to drop me in the shit.'

'Yeah, I'll be careful. I have spoken to the pathologist at the morgue. Juliet Edgar was very helpful. It appears the paperwork from the first post-mortem wasn't completed properly. Something to do with the drug data analysis being missing. I understand your Metropolitan Police boyfriend had also been there checking it out.'

'My what?'

'Your fancy man, Jim Green.'

'Don't worry about him. He's history. I've been seeing someone else since him. You know me, I don't hang about.'

'So, who is it this time? Another policeman?'

'That local councillor, Toby Brown. I only went with him for about a week. Too full of himself, and he drinks more than you. He didn't cut the mustard with me.'

'Blue, green, brown. All the colours of the rainbow. Which colour are you going to pick next?'

'Brown isn't a colour in the rainbow, you prat!'

'Okay, I get it!' I said, realising the conversation was becoming childish and overheated.

'Mm, this tea's gone cold,' said Sue.

'Too much talking. Would you like me to pour you another?' I asked.

'No. I best be going. It's a tad busy down the nick.'

'Okay.'

'Just quickly, how are you doing? Are you off the booze yet?'

'Have a look around. You won't find a bottle anywhere.'

'I bet you've been to the pub!'

'I can't lie.'

'You had better not. I'm a police officer, remember!'

'Oh, handcuffs. Oops!'

'You don't help yourself, do you? Why start something you can't finish?' said Sue, rolling her eyes.

'I'm on the case with that one, trust me.'

'If you want me, you had better be quick. Once more for old time's sake and all that.'

'Not going to happen.'

'Why?'

'You know why. I'm not going to put myself through all that again.'

‘Daniel, Hun. You do know I didn’t mean to hurt you. How was I to know you would fall stupidly in love with me? Most other men just want a quick fuck, and then they’re off. That is where I underestimated you.’

‘Because I thought I had fallen in love?’

‘Yes, well, and you know what thought did!’

‘Thankfully, I’ve had time to think. I won’t put myself in that situation again.’

‘Another thing...’

‘What?’

‘You need to get your ex, Lianna, out of your system. When I was with you, all I heard was, “Lianna this, and Lianna that.” It’s not good to hear, and it certainly shattered any true feelings I may have had for you. Remember, relationships are not just all one-way traffic. Despite what you think, I have a heart and still have space for you in there somewhere. Fuck knows why?’

‘Sorry, I didn’t mean to get into an argument.’

‘Daniel, love. It's not an argument. It’s a much-needed frank discussion.’

‘Yeah, I know!’

‘I need to go now. Keep your chin up. We’re still friends, aren’t we?’

‘You’re always asking me that!’

‘It’s because I care about you. That’s why!’

‘Thank you!’

‘I’ll buzz you when I hear more about Iona and the case. Just stay low for a while. Promise?’

‘Yes, I promise.’

14

One of the niggling things about becoming a freelance reporter is the lack of routine. As much as I try to stick to a diary or timeline, everything is sporadic—days when I'm busy and even more days when I'm not. The last week has been too quiet. Money worries have forced me to reach for the bottle again. The saving grace is that I cannot afford to carry on drinking, so my current alcohol experience is somewhat curtailed.

Looking back through some old emails, I realised I'd missed a couple of appointments: a follow-up with the doctor and a blood test with the nurse. Why is it these appointments are always on the days I'm busy?

Just when I thought it would be another day of moping around, I received a text message from Sue. Iona Turner was out of intensive care and sitting up on the ward. I somehow felt obliged to give Sue a ring.

'Sue, it's Daniel.'

'Yes, I can see. I take it you've seen my text.'

'Is Iona alright?'

'As right as she can be, considering. I visited her yesterday, and she was able to give a statement.'

'Does she know who attacked her?'

'No, unfortunately. Iona said she heard a rumbling sound, turned, and saw the well cover had come open and was clouted from behind. For some reason, she thinks her attacker was female, though.'

'Why?'

'Iona said she smelt perfume. It's the last thing she remembers before waking up in the hospital.'

'Flipping heck.'

'And another thing, Oh, and I haven't told you this.'

'What?'

'We had the results back from Forensics. The only DNA and human blood they found was Iona's.'

'Why do you say human blood?'

‘The other samples they found belonged to an animal. Probably a fox, it says in their report.’

‘What about fingerprints?’

‘After eliminating Iona’s and those of the other neighbour, there weren’t any.’

‘Could the other neighbour, what’s his name? Could he be the culprit?’

‘Mr Peters? No, we were able to rule him out very early on.’

‘That’s one thing, I suppose. Is Iona allowed any visitors?’

‘Her son arrived yesterday, just as we were leaving, so yes, I guess so. Please, though, remember to keep a low profile.’

‘Okay, thanks. I will.’

‘And… if she says anything I haven’t already told you, can you let me know?’

‘Yes, of course.’

‘Good, then you can tell me over a drink.’

‘Ha, ha. Stop trying to catch me out.’

‘Freudian slip, that’s all.’

‘Freudian, my ass!’

Sue laughed and put the phone down. It was time for me to jump on a train and get over to Frimley.

It was quite a wet and windy day, so on arrival, I quickly popped into the gents to sort myself out before enquiring where Iona was.

Eventually, I found her sitting in a chair in the corner by the window, reading a book of poems.

‘Hello, dear, you should read this.’

‘What is it?’

‘Background Music by Christy Brown.’

‘He’s Irish, isn’t he?’

‘I think so, but he’s been dead for a good while. Google it!’ said Iona, laughing.

‘Somehow, I knew you were going to say that! So, tell me how you are?’

‘I’m okay. I think they’ll let me go home in a couple of days. They need to do a few more checks and get my blood pressure back up first.’

‘Will you feel safe at home?’

‘Oh yes, I’ve arranged for my sister, Margaret, to stay. She popped in to see me earlier and grabbed a key. She came all the way down from Knott-End-on-Sea.’

‘Where’s that?’

‘Up north, somewhere near Blackpool. She married someone from there she met whilst on her hols some years back.’

‘Oh, I see. Oh, here’s some flowers, by the way.’

‘£7.49 from Waitrose, Oh, you shouldn’t have,’ said Iona picking at the cellophane.

‘Whoops. I hope you like them, though.’

‘Of course, thank you. Geraniums are my favourite.’

‘I understand the police came to see you yesterday.’

‘Oh yes, dear. Your friend DI Grendel and some other gormless copper.’

‘So, you were able to tell them what happened?’

‘Yes, but not all of it.’

‘What do you mean?’

‘If I had told them everything, they would never have believed me.’

‘Why?’

‘Whatever attacked me wasn’t of this world,’ said Iona, lowering her voice.

‘What do you mean?’

‘Ever since that day I took you into Ms Babineaux’s house, things have changed. It’s as if we disturbed something. I’ve felt an eerie presence ever since. That wasn’t a person who whacked me over the head. It was something else!’

‘Not a person? What then?’

‘I am sure it was a poltergeist.’

‘What?’

‘I did turn and see, but I couldn’t tell your police lady friend yesterday. She would have thought I was nuts.’

‘Such things don’t exist, do they?’

‘Trust me, until this happened, I didn’t believe in things that go bump in the night. But this happened. The ghost of Virna Babineaux attacked me.’

‘Really? That’s a wild statement!’

‘You don’t believe me, do you?’

‘How do you know it was Virna?’

'I could see her snarling face in the manifestation each time it spun around.'

'What?'

'And her hair, those long blond locks of hers, were flailing. It was her alright. And then, in a flash, she was gone.'

'And then you woke up here?'

'Yes, dear.'

'Are you sure it wasn't a dream? Remember, you had taken a nasty blow to the head, and you've been on some heavy medication.'

'That had crossed my mind, but then I thought about the smell. You can't smell in dreams, can you?'

'I thought you could.'

'Anyway, I smelt perfume. The same perfume Ms Babineaux used to wear. Black Opium. It has a distinctive smell to it.'

'Flipping heck. I can now understand why you didn't tell Sue all this.'

'The other police officer who came yesterday, I can't remember his name now. He said something about Forensics not finding anything. He received a message moments before they left here. That would prove I'm telling the truth, wouldn't it?'

'You're the retired police officer, so I'm sure you would like to think so, wouldn't you?'

'Of course.'

'All I'll say now is, there must be a rational explanation.'

'There you go again. You don't believe me, do you?'

'Iona, I'm trying to believe you, but none of this is adding up.'

The conversation was abruptly halted by a nurse who wanted to get Iona back to bed ready for a transfer to another ward.

'Thank you for coming to see me and for the lovely flowers,' said Iona as I stepped back to give the nurse some room. 'You will come and see me for a cuppa when I'm back home, won't you?'

'Yes, Iona, I will. Thanks!'

On leaving the ward, the nurse followed me into the corridor.

'Do you know Mrs Turner well? I overheard parts of the conversation. You're not family, are you?' she whispered.

'No, but I've known Iona since I was a child. She was good friends with my late mum.'

‘Oh, I see. Sorry. I was with a doctor yesterday who discussed Mrs Turner’s injury. The blow to her head was only superficial. A mere scratch. It would not have been enough to put her in hospital.’

‘So why is she here?’

‘Dr Rebus believes Mrs Turner is suffering from something called phantosmia. A head injury could have caused it. Most likely, though, it’s been caused by an upper respiratory infection. You can see Mrs Turner is getting on in years, so simple ageing could be the root cause.’

‘She’s only sixty-seven though, isn’t she? That’s not that old!’

‘She’s of pensionable age. The ageing process affects everyone differently. We’re also checking for any lobe seizures, inflamed sinuses and brain tumours. We see that she was admitted to St Peter's hospital in Chertsey with Covid-19 in 2020, which could be another reason for her current condition.’

‘Oh, I see. I understand Iona’s son visited yesterday. Would he be aware of all this?’

‘He didn’t stay much longer than five minutes, but he did speak with Dr Rebus, so he should be aware, yes!’

‘Okay, good. Thanks.’

Travelling back, I kept thinking about what Iona said about a poltergeist attacking her. Police forensics didn’t find anything which would support her story. Speaking to the nurse at least gave me a rational explanation for everything. Now though, I had Bill Pattenden’s voice ringing in my head, ‘Don’t forget the basics. Don’t forget the basics!’

Ah, Mr Peters. He’s the one who found Iona and called for an ambulance. Sue said he was eliminated from the police enquiries very early on. I now convinced myself something might have been missed. Does this Mr Peters know more than he’s been letting on?

Peters. Littlewick Road. Knaphill. Woking. Found him. Google does the trick again. I couldn’t help smiling as I thought about Iona’s would-be reaction if she knew.

Alwyn Peters. Forty-six years old, married with a disabled wife. She appears much younger. He works as her carer. Interests: N/A. He must be interested in something, so I widened my search. Bi-sexual. Former mental health patient.

Schizophrenia. He used to belong to an amateur dramatic society, and then BINGO! I found a photograph of him standing outside a shop in London. Although the picture appears to have been taken a few years ago, the caption underneath says, 'an enjoyable afternoon shopping at Honour.' I couldn't help thinking he looked familiar.

'Honour' is a sex shop, in Lower Marsh, around the corner from Waterloo Station. It's also close to Roupell Street, where Virna was murdered. Apart from being her neighbour in Knaphill, I sensed there was possibly another connection. I now hoped Alwyn Peters was prepared to talk. I knew I would need to speak to him urgently before Iona came out of the hospital.

15

It was one of those rare mornings I felt motivated, and my urge to visit Mr Peters and speak to him before Iona came out of the hospital was paramount. I wanted to know his version of events before the pair had an opportunity to talk to each other.

I decided to ride down on my Harley, it had been a few months, and I felt it was time to give it an airing and a good check over before its MOT in a couple of weeks. Riding a top-range motorbike with a pesky Jameson's habit doesn't mix, so I knew in this respect I was being sensible by keeping it mothballed in the shed.

I parked up by the front gate and walked along a gravel path. I saw a woman about thirty-something in a wheelchair through the front room window. After a couple of rings, the door was eventually answered.

'Hello, can I help you?'

'Alwyn Peters?'

'Yes, that's right. Are you the police?'

'No,' I said, reeling back. 'Do I know you from a previous life?'

'You look familiar? Daniel, isn't it? You used to drink in The Anchor up the hill, a few years back.'

'Yes, I thought I recognised you.'

'And you say you're not the police.'

'No, definitely not.'

'Thank God for that, so what are you these days?'

'I'm a reporter.'

'Jesus Christ. That's even worse.'

'Why do you say that?'

'I've had so many visits recently. My wife has become so anxious. The police keep asking questions about the house next door.'

'Yes, I know. I understand it was you who found Iona Turner.'

'I did.'

'Do you know who attacked her?'

‘Shush! Can we go outside and talk about this? I don’t want the wife overhearing.’

Alwyn took me around the side of the house. We then sat at a table by a pond at the bottom of the garden.

‘I’ve been to see Iona. She’s okay. She’s hoping to be home in a couple of days.’

‘You know Iona?’

‘She was a friend of my mother's. Mum died a few years ago.’

‘Oh. Sorry.’

‘So, you found Iona lying on the ground. Tell me what happened.’

‘What has Iona told you?’

‘Enough, well, everything, hopefully.’

‘Oh, God. Oh, no, no, no,’ said Alwyn, shaking.

‘If you don’t mind me saying. You seem a little nervous.’

‘I knew this was all going to come out. I just knew it.’

‘What?’

‘Me and Iona.’

‘Hang on, isn’t Iona old enough to be your mother?’

‘Yes, and that was part of the thrill.’

‘What thrill?’

‘Going upstairs, next door.’

‘In Virna Babineaux’s house?’ I asked hesitantly.

‘Yes.’

‘Where, upstairs?’

‘In the attic.’

‘Oh, I see.’

‘I don’t think you do. Do you know what’s up there?’

‘Yes, I do. Iona took me up there when she showed me around the house back in September.’

‘Jesus Christ. So, she’s told you?’

‘Go on...’

‘Iona and I went in the house most Wednesday evenings when my wife was out playing bingo. Someone from the charity used to pick her up and take her to the Gala place in Reading. She’d be gone for a good three or four hours.’

‘So, what was going on between you and Iona.’

‘I’m assuming Iona has told you now anyway.’

‘Carry on.’

‘A few months after I heard the French lady got murdered, I realised no-one was going into the house. I had heard on the grapevine there was no family around. I found my way in through a tunnel in the garden. I’d known it had been there since I was a child. We used to play there a long time ago. It was before the original owners moved away.’

‘Flipping heck.’

‘At first, I found lots of wine in the cellar and would sit down there drinking while Lucy, my wife, was at bingo.’

‘Then what?’

‘It went on for a few months. I got to love the place. I had so many good childhood memories of playing in there when we were all still children. I realised no-one was coming to the house apart from the postman. I found out someone was paying Iona to look after the place and keep it clean.’

‘Iona?’

‘Yes.’

‘Are you sure? She says she doesn’t know who’s been going in the house.’

‘She doesn’t want anyone to know. I’m not sure why. I always picked the flowers from the garden and gave them to Iona. She would place them in the front window of the house to give the impression someone was still living there.’

‘So why has Iona been lying to me?’

‘Can we not talk about that?’

‘Come on. You’ve told me lots already. I may as well hear the rest.’

‘It’s all quite embarrassing, but you may as well hear my version of events. None of this must reach Lucy, mind.’

‘Don’t worry, your secret’s safe with me.’

At last, I felt I was getting somewhere. I had purposely held back from talking about Iona too much as it appeared Alwyn had the impression that she had already told me everything. It was a ploy Bill Pattenden once taught me. Open questioning, I think he called it.

‘I noticed Lucy is in a wheelchair. I saw her through the window as I rang your doorbell.’

‘She fell off her horse in a riding accident about twelve years ago. She’s been paralysed from the waist down ever since.’

‘I’m sorry. So, about Iona, what is your version of things?’

‘It’s all about the attic room. After about a year, I felt comfortable going into the house, always via the tunnel. No-one else would have known it was there. Even Lucy doesn’t know about it. As you would have seen, there’s quite a lot of kinky stuff up there. I had found not being able to have sex with Lucy anymore quite frustrating. I couldn’t go out and find anyone else as I had to be here for Lucy. In the end, I began to satisfy myself with all the dildos and other toys up there.’

‘Whoops, too much information. So, what does Iona have to do with all this?’

‘One evening, I was up there and heard a noise. I was petrified. I had dressed myself up in some black lingerie and fishnet stockings. I thought it was someone from the Babineaux family. The more I tried to be quiet, the more noise I made. Suddenly, the door flung open, and it was Iona. She had let herself in.’

‘Oh dear, oh dear, oh dear,’ I said, trying my hardest not to laugh.

‘She’s probably told you I tried to bribe her not to tell anyone, but it’s the other way around.’

‘Go on.’

‘Iona said she’d tell Lucy and the whole village about what she saw unless….’

‘Unless?’

‘Unless I agreed to meet her there every Wednesday while Lucy was playing bingo.’

‘That I do find hard to believe. Iona is in her late-sixties, isn’t she?’

‘She’s sixty-seven.’

‘And you?’

‘I’m forty-six. I find Iona very sexy, and she is quite a good-looking woman, despite her age.’

‘So, you and I are about the same age, and you’re letting yourself get involved with someone old enough to be your mother? What did Iona want with you?’

‘We spoke about it a few times, and she said she was quite turned on by what she saw. It reminded her of her good times when she was younger.’

'That must be a policewoman thing,' I said, thinking about my time with Sue.

'What?'

'Sorry, it doesn't matter.'

'Iona wanted me to dress up. There are plenty of uniforms. She'd wear one of the long curly wigs and whip me. Always on my lower back and the back of my legs until I was red raw.'

'Did Iona dress up?'

'Apart from wearing a wig, no. She always wore her black leather trousers and a white blouse. She wanted to be the cruel schoolmistress, especially when I wore the schoolgirl's outfit. Then, she loved wearing a vibrating strap-on.'

'Oh, again, too much information. Stop! I think it's best if we leave it there. At least I think I've solved the mystery of the fresh flowers and the nice clean house. I can't believe you've told me all this.'

'Well, Iona has told you anyway.'

'Clearly not all, not about the kinky stuff, she didn't. And I can't believe she's lying. Why report it all to the police when it's been her going into the house and replacing the flowers all along?'

'I don't know, but I do know her mind wanders sometimes.'

'I don't doubt it. It just confirms something a nurse said about Iona at the hospital.'

'What?'

'No, don't worry, it's nothing. It's all a bit strange, that's all. It appears you assumed I knew everything, so you told me anyway. It's an old policeman's trick.'

'You said you weren't a policeman.'

'I'm not. I'm a freelance investigative journalist working for myself. I think your nerves got the better of you. You just wanted to spurt everything out and get it off your chest.'

'Mm, perhaps you're right.'

'I know I am. Now, going back to my original question. Do you know who attacked Iona?'

'It wasn't me if that's what you're thinking. It wasn't anything.'

'Explain.'

‘I had moved the concrete cover in the garden for Iona as usual. I was already in the cellar pouring myself a glass of wine. For some reason, everything went stone cold. I’d never felt anything like it before. Not in all the time I’d been going in the house. There was a whoosh-like sound and then a squeal. Everything went foggy for a few split-seconds as the cellar light dimmed.’

‘Then what?’

‘Once I had gathered my senses, I rushed into the tunnel and then outside. Iona was lying on the ground, semi-conscious and holding her head. There was blood everywhere. Lots of it! Iona passed out, so I dialled 999 and then rushed back down to seal the cellar.’

‘Iona told me she thinks a poltergeist attacked her,’ I said.

‘Whatever it was, it wasn’t human.’

‘Fucking hell. Sorry. You actually think it was a ghost or spirit as well?’

‘I smelt the perfume. It was the same as the French lady used to wear.’

‘Black Opium?’

‘I don’t know what it’s called. It’s the first time I had smelt it since she died.’

‘Alwyn, everything you’ve told me has blown me away. I wasn’t expecting you to say so much.’

‘Nor was I. As you said, I think I just needed to get it off my chest. I can hardly tell Lucy, can I?

‘I guess we’ve all been there in our own different ways.’

‘Promise you won’t print anything.’

‘I don’t usually make promises. Anyway, the focus now is to find out who’s paying all the bills on Virna’s house. The money must be coming from somewhere. Do you know?’

‘I don’t, no.’

‘I didn’t think so. Did you know Virna’s body had gone missing from a mortuary?’

‘That, I didn’t. I thought there would have been a funeral years ago.’

‘Apparently not.’

‘Do you know if the police are coming back? Lucy won’t like that.’

‘I doubt it. For some reason, DI Grendel told me you had been eliminated from their enquiries quite early on. Don’t worry. I won’t tell them anything.’

‘Good. What about Iona?’

‘That, my friend, is for you to sort out.’

After getting back home, I tried to reassess everything Alwyn had told me. I hardly believed my luck, but most importantly, remembering to use the open-questioning technique, which Bill had taught me all those years ago, got me some mighty fine answers.

16

Usually, when I dream, I wake up in the morning and can't remember anything. Sometimes, I remember snippets, then wonder what the hell it was all about. Last night was different. I've woken up and placed everything in fine detail. I can only put it down to my research and what happened to Virna. After looking at all those exotic pictures, I was now worried I had become besotted with her.

In the dream, I found myself in a boudoir along a street in Pigalle, Paris. It was in the shadow of the imposing Sacré-Cœur basilica.

The room was dimly lit, but I could see everything. There was a distinctive smell of candle wax and incense—another, of an Indian oil-based perfume.

I kept asking where I was. Who was there? At first, I had no answer. All I could hear were the bells from the basilica. Eventually, I could see the silhouette of a tall woman standing over me.

'Hello, my inadequate English friend,' she said. 'Kneel!'

The next thing I was on my knees on a cold tiled black stone floor, naked, hands bound with rope behind my back. The woman raised her right arm. In her hand was a long leather strap.

Lash, lash, lash.

She pounded it across my lower back. I didn't flinch, even though my back was sore.

It came again, *lash, lash, lash.*

She clutched my hair and turned me round, forcing the leather-gloved index finger of her left hand into my mouth.

'There, suck' she demanded. This went on for about ten minutes.

'Suck, suck,' she yelled, pushing it further down my throat.

I began to choke as I turned to look at her face.

'Don't look at me, you worm,' she shouted, as she forced my head away.

Her eyes were covered with a black lace mask. Her hair was long and blond. Her shoulders were bare, and she was dressed in a black leather corset, with black fish-net stockings and high-length matching boots with red laces.

'There, there, my disgusting little English worm,' she uttered as she moved me back to where I was. At last, I was able to breathe again.

And then it came once more. *Lash, lash, lash.* This time, I flinched.

'Rouge, jaune, verte,' she whispered.

'Green,' I cried. For some reason, I didn't want her to stop.

And again, *lash, lash, lash* until there was a period of complete silence.

'Come, lay down, my little sissy, worm,' she murmured as she freed my hands from behind my back.

'You like what you see?' she asked.

'Yes!'

'Do you worship me?'

I hesitated.

'Well, my little English worm? Answer me!'

'Ah, yes, I like you very much.'

'Not good enough. You MUST call me Mistress! Understand?'

'Yes, Mistress.'

'DO YOU WORSHIP ME?'

'Yes, yes, Mistress.'

'Good. You like this?' she asked, as she pushed me back down, forcing a cold metal clasp around my testicles.

'I'm not sure,' I said, as I became tense and nervous.

'He, he, Worm. Do not worry. I promise you will like it later,' she laughed.

'I hope so,' I said nervously as I felt the clasp getting tighter.

'Your little dinky. Is it a good boy? I want to see it big. Let it grow big,' she demanded as she reached for a horsewhip from a rack on the wall behind my head.

There was no hiding place.

'Come on, let me see it grow,' she shouted as she tightened up the clasp even more and lightly whipped my penis. 'There, there, how you say in English? Oh, yes, yes, yes. I can now see signs of life in your pathetic excuse for a dinky now.'

She was right. There were signs of life. I began to relax a little. She grabbed my hand and placed it on my cock.

'There, now slowly, stroke, stroke it, that's it, my clever little English worm. Play!'

I felt her get closer. I could smell stale tobacco on her breath. Below her mask, I could see her lips, full, red, pouting.

'Do you want me to fuck?'

'Pardon?'

'Do you want me to fuck?'

'Oh, yes, Mistress, yes please, please!'

'My little inadequate worm. Stroke, stroke. Come on, harder, faster,' she demanded as she pulled her head away.

Just then, she put a damp white hand towel over my eyes.

'Don't touch, don't take it off, you must stop looking at me,' she ordered.

I felt her leather glove move up between my legs and under my balls. I heard the cap come off a plastic bottle.

'Don't move, worm,' she whispered.

And then, I felt the cold sensation of lubrication gel being applied around my ass. She then removed the clasp from my balls.

'Now, keep stroking, harder, faster, faster, come on, come on!'

I heard a click. I wasn't sure what it was.

'Come on, harder, faster, harder, faster. I want you to come, come, come.'

The more I tried, the more difficult it became. My cock was hard, but nothing would spurt out.

'You are a stubborn little English worm, aren't you? AREN'T YOU!' she shouted.

'Yes, Mistress, yes, yes.'

And then there was a thrust, as I felt a large pulsating object slither up my ass.

'Now worm, come, come COME!' she demanded.

The hand towel slipped.

As she pushed the dildo back and forth with her right hand, I could see she was pleasuring herself with the left.

'Come, come, come,' she screamed.

Now, I realised she was also talking to herself. I heard screams of delight. The more she screamed, the more confident I felt that I was about to come. The sensation of that final jerk before ejaculation was becoming more imminent.

'Come, come, come,' she continued.

And then it did. That moment of satisfaction. Self-gratification. The final shudder. I was breathless and in a sweat.

'Espèce de merde anglaise sans valeur!' she said,

I wasn't sure what she was saying. She then stood up, 'What have you done? What have you done?' she yelped.

I remained silent.

'Worm,' she shouted.

I felt myself smiling awkwardly as I admired the full view of her exquisite body.

'Would you like to look deep into my eyes now?' she asked, reaching for her mask.

'Yes, Mistress, yes, yes,' I eagerly replied, as I imagined something of impeccable beauty.

As she removed her mask, she spun round and hissed violently. Her face became skeletal as her whole body morphed into something not of this world.

'*Fugazi*, *Fugazi*, *FUGAZI*,' she screamed.

I was now faced with a looming spectre hovering over me. In absolute shock, I reeled away.

'*FUGAZI*!'

When I turned and looked again, there was nothing, not one shred of evidence from what I had just experienced. All I could hear was the continuous sound of bells tolling solemnly from the basilica. I couldn't explain it. Daylight was coming in through the shutters.

I then stood and looked into a mirror. It wasn't easy separating the dream from reality. A sense of innate fear remained until I was sure I was fully awake and back in the land of the living.

Why, oh, why had I been dreaming about Virna? Was it Virna?

Later, in self-analysis, I recognised my mind was playing tricks. My subconscious was fighting against all the negativity in my sex life. I had somehow become submissive. A worm indeed.

Not something I should utter to anyone, even though I found some strange comfort in the experience.

17

This morning I received an unexpected text message from Annie: 'Hey, my lovely, it's Annie. How are you? It would be great to catch up sometime. Give me a call. I have a little something for you.' At first, I felt apprehensive, but curiosity got the better of me, so I made contact. We arranged to meet at Bernie Spain Gardens on the Southbank in London, where we had been before.

Having made the journey to London, it was now late afternoon, an hour or so before dark on the first Friday in November. After a few weeks of mild weather, temperatures had begun to drop considerably and for once, I was starting to feel the cold. I sat on the bench where we were last time and waited for Annie to arrive.

'Hello, my lovely, long time no see. How are you?'

'Okay, I think. How about you?'

'Yes, I'm alright. It could be better. You know. Life is what it is.'

'Tell me about it. Anyway, I never thought I would see you again. Your text this morning came as a complete surprise.'

'In all honesty, I've been a little bored and lonely of late. I remembered your case and started browsing the internet to see if I could find out more about what had happened to Virna.'

'And?'

'Well, I did. I decided to look outside the box, and Robert Surcouf's name kept popping up. The original Robert Surcouf was born in St Malo, France 1773. He was a ship owner and prominent slave trader. He became famous for plundering American and British merchant ships during his lifetime, and the French loved him for it. He was something of a hero. He died when he was fifty-three in 1827.'

'Mm, what has all this got to do with the Robert Surcouf who killed Virna, though?'

'It's a loose connection, my lovely, but I think it is important. The guy who murdered Virna was originally called Robert Gross. Surcouf was his boyhood hero. He'd read many books about him whilst growing up and became groomed by some of Surcouf's ideologies before adopting his name in the late 1990s.'

'How do you know all this?'

'Around the time Surcouf was convicted for Virna's Murder, some stuff appeared on the internet. It was all in French, so I had to translate it. The Surcouf name stood out, drawing my attention.'

'Flipping heck, you are clever,'

'Not really, oh, and that's not all.'

'What?'

'I also found out that there's a direct connection between Surcouf and Jonathan Blackwell. He's the artist, isn't he?'

'Yes.'

'By 2004, Surcouf was now living in England. The post on the internet suggests he had moved so he could be with his lover, referred to as VB. I'm guessing that would be Virna Babineaux.'

'Sounds good.'

'Surcouf came to England, intent on killing Jonathan Blackwell. He had discovered Virna and Jonathan had fallen in love.'

'What? How come I didn't see any of this? I did plenty of internet searches.'

'Did you search for Robert Surcouf or William Kuznia?' asked Annie.

'No, I don't think I did.'

'Well, fortunately, I did. As I said, it was all in French, and the only reference to Virna was VB. I doubt if you would have ever found it. Well, I told you I was bored.'

'You said Surcouf wanted to murder Jonathan?'

'Yes, I did. Jonathan was stabbed in the shoulder after putting up a good fight. He was hospitalised and released after a couple of days. Surcouf fled back to France using his own name, Gross, to avoid arrest. As he was never apprehended for stabbing Jonathan, it never went to court. If it had, we would have discovered what we need to know much sooner.'

'Yet, when he was arrested for killing Virna, he was arrested as Robert Surcouf.'

'He must have had paperwork to support that. That probably suited him. It's just that when he was arrested for killing Virna, the police were probably not aware he was living under a false name. From what I can tell, any reference to Gross during the murder trial never came up.'

'So, where do you think this new information will take me now?'

'To be honest, I don't know. I found it, and I felt it was only right to share it with you.'

'Thank you. I'm glad you got bored!'

Annie chuckled. 'Come on. It's getting cold and dark. You look like you need a drink. Let's go to the film institute under the bridge. They have a nice bar in there. You still drink, don't you?' she said, shivering.

'Err, yes. Sometimes,' I said reluctantly.

When we arrived, I grabbed a table in the corner while Annie went to the bar.

'There you go, my lovely. One large whiskey.'

'Thank you. What the hell is that you're drinking?'

'It's a Negroni.'

'A what?'

'Negroni. It consists of gin, vermouth, and Campari, all in equal measures.'

'Never heard of it.'

'Then you haven't lived,' said Annie as she offered me a sip.

'Anyway. I must ask. What happened between you and Bill Pattenden?'

'Ha, ha. I'm surprised you haven't asked me that already.'

I smiled. 'Let's just say I was waiting for the right moment.'

'It was all a bit silly. Me and my big mouth and all that.'

'Bill said something along those lines.'

'What did he tell you?'

'Something about a breach of confidentiality.'

'It wasn't that exactly.'

'What was it then?'

'It's a very long story.'

'It doesn't need to be. Just give me the bullet points.'

'Well, Bill treated me like he was my Sugar Daddy. I loved all the attention. He'd take me out, and we'd go to the best restaurants, cinema and business functions. He liked nothing more than having a young lady on his arm. He loved showing me off to his friends from the masonic lodge and all their associates.'

'So why did he sack you?'

'Actually, it wasn't the sack. Bill said he had to let me go. It was about his wife. She had become suspicious of our activities. He wasn't telling her anything. One day I spoke to him without realising. She was standing right behind me in the office. It was the day I went down to Camberley for my appraisal.'

'Oh. What did you say?'

'It's best if I don't tell you anything else. I've told you enough already.'

'Annie, you have to tell me. I must confess. I know things that perhaps you think I don't know.'

'What things, my lovely?'

'You see that little scorpion you have tattooed on your wrist.'

'This one?' said Annie pulling back the sleeve on her right arm.

'Yes, that one.'

'What about it?'

'Whilst it's a very nice tattoo, it's been letting you down quite badly.'

'How? What do you mean?'

'I mean, it's led me to find out about all your extracurricular activities. I know about the S&M bondage thing.'

'You've been checking me out?'

'Accidentally, yes, I suppose so. I know you and Bill were up to things. Curiosity killed the cat and all that. Yes, I looked. Even I look outside the box sometimes.'

'What have you seen?'

'Well, I've seen the pictures. Even though your face was obscured, I immediately recognised the tattoo. Part of me wanted to believe what I saw, but part of me didn't. In the end, I realised it was none of my business.'

'Now you disapprove. Now you don't like me.'

'If I didn't like you, I wouldn't have come to London today to see you.'

'Yes, but I said I had something for you. That's how men are so easily trapped. You mentioned curiosity. Was it curiosity that brought you here?'

'Yes, well, if I'm honest, yes!'

'Then my little ploy worked. Another whiskey?'

'It's alright. I'll get the drinks this time. What's yours called again?'

'Negroni.'

When I returned from the bar, Annie had gone. 'It's alright,' said a young girl sitting opposite. 'She's said she's only going to powder her nose.' I sat alone with our drinks for a good ten minutes before Annie reappeared. She had now taken her hair down from the top of her head and had applied fresh makeup and perfume.

'There, I feel like a real woman again now. I needed that.'

'I'm sure you did. You look nice.'

'Thank you. I like a bit of flattery,'

'Don't worry, that's only the drink talking.'

'Oh, go on and spoil it, why don't you,' said Annie, twiddling with a strand of hair that had fallen across her face.

'Ha, ha. Sorry. I didn't mean to. Anyway, talking of being curious, tell me more about what you've been up to?'

'No, not here. It's gone a bit quiet. Let's finish our drinks, and we can talk about it on the way to the station. I've got to get the tube to Kennington, and you, my lovely, want to catch a train to Woking, don't you?'

'Yes.'

We stepped out into the cold night. It was getting late, and I was trying to work out the time of my last train home. Annie had locked her arm inside mine as we walked along the Thames towpath along the Southbank towards Waterloo. She kept looking up at me and smiling. By the time we reached the station, neither of us had uttered a word.

'There we go, we're here,' said Annie.

'I know.'

'I'll wait with you for a few minutes until your train to Woking comes in. Is that alright?'

'Yes, of course.'

'Let's go and stand under the clock. It's supposed to be one of the most romantic places in the country,' said Annie, grasping my hand. 'We'll wait here until we know which platform you need.'

What worried me was that all the passenger information boards were blank. A woman's voice on the public address system was muffled. I couldn't hear a thing. It became apparent that no trains were entering or leaving the station. After a while, I realised I might be stranded. The next train popped up on the screen, but it wasn't going until 01.05. That was a two-hour wait!

'Come on,' said Annie. 'Come back to mine. I'm not waiting around that long. Besides, I have a tube to catch. Come on. I promise I won't bite.'

'Are you sure?'

'Sure, I want you to come with me, or sure that I don't bite?'

'Both, I suppose.'

Annie's place was a short walk from Kennington tube station into Cornwall Street.

'Hang on. I'll put the heating on and fix us a drink,' she said just after we got inside.'

'A very nice place, clean and tidy.'

'It has to be. Clients and all that. Before you ask, the equipment room is through there,' she said, pointing. 'Go on, look. Don't worry. I promise I won't follow you.'

Everything resembled what I had seen in Virna's house in Knaphill a few weeks ago.

'What's your favourite? What do you like best? You must have seen something you like.'

'I've seen all this on your web page. I've very recently had dreams about this sort of thing, but I'm not sure if I want to try it.'

'Don't worry. I can tell it's not for you. If it were, you would have been expecting me to drag you in there already.'

'Do you actually have sex with all the men?'

'Obvious question, but no, never. I refer to myself, and myself only, as The Virgin Prostitute. I never have penetrative sex, never do oral or even hand relief. If one of my clients wants to toss himself off at £300 an hour, he's welcome to,' said Annie laughing.

'£300 an hour?'

'That's my going rate. On average, I do one to twelve clients each month, and one is the same guy over three visits. It's better than working for a living, although I would prefer to make my living as a journalist.'

'And what about security? Do you feel safe?'

'Oh, very. Storm, she's the butch lesbian next door. I text her when someone I don't know is about to arrive. She's an ex-army girl and a black belt in karate. You wouldn't want to argue with her.'

'Do you pay her?'

'Let's just say she likes a good whipping.'

I laughed. 'Good. I'm glad you feel safe.'

'You sound like you care?'

'I think what you do is scary, intriguing nonetheless, but you're also quite vulnerable.'

'Oh, my lovely, You're very sweet. Look, I said I don't bite. Would you mind using the spare room? It's all made up. Now, get a good night's sleep and then we can go for breakfast somewhere in the morning.'

The evening seemed to come to quite an abrupt end, but for all the right reasons. There was something about Annie I was beginning to like. She certainly was one of the most interesting and exciting people I had ever met.

18

It had been a few days since I'd seen Annie, and I was finding it difficult to get her out of my mind. Perhaps I was fantasising too much. The main thing was the information she gave me might be helpful. Robert Surcouf stabbing Jonathan Blackwell? I still can't believe that went under the radar. And why wasn't Surcouf convicted of Virna's murder under his real name Gross? I can't believe the police missed that. Indeed, they must have known his real name. I'll ask Sue about the protocol when I next speak to her.

I was just getting my head around things when there was a loud bang on the front door.

'Daniel Blue? Mister Daniel Lionel Blue?'

'Yes, that's my name.'

'Can we come in?' said the woman showing me a police identity card. 'I'm DCI Jacqui Boast, and this is my colleague Sergeant Grant Fellows.'

'What's this all about?'

'Mr Blue, you have become a person of interest to us,' she said.

'Why?'

'I understand you are familiar with a case currently under investigation.'

'Virna Babineaux?'

'Yes, that one.'

'I thought it had been dropped.'

'What makes you think that?'

'My friend Sue, she's one of your lot. She told me the police weren't interested anymore.'

'Oh, Mr Blue, we are very much still interested. This Sue, what's her full name?'

'Sue Grendel. Detective Inspector Sue Grendel.'

'Surrey Police?'

'Yes.'

'Mr Blue, we're from the Metropolitan Police Force. We've received information that on Wednesday, 21st of September, you visited the West London Morgue, giving the staff the impression, you were a police officer.'

'No. Absolutely not. Categorically not so. I made it perfectly clear I was an investigative journalist following a lead relating to a missing body.'

'Mr Blue, I personally spoke to the receptionist, Miss Daloney Moore, yesterday afternoon, who was adamant you were passing yourself off as a police officer.'

'Not true. Have you spoken to Juliet Edgar? She's the person who helped me with some of the information I was looking for. She will confirm I'm telling the truth. She even took the mickey when I told her I was a reporter.'

'Don't worry, Mr Blue, I shall. What role does Juliet Edgar have at the morgue?'

'I believe she's the senior forensic pathologist. Surely, it's her who you should have spoken to, not the fucking receptionist.'

'Now, now, Mr Blue. Don't get lairy with us. There's no need.'

'Of course, there is a need. You've come barging into my house, accusing me of impersonating a police officer, which simply isn't true.'

'A point of fact, Mr Blue. We showed you our ID. I politely asked if we could come in. You stepped aside and showed us right here into your front room.'

'Okay, okay. Sarcasm, now, is it? I suggest you both leave.'

After they'd left, I realised not once did they ask me about what information I had gathered. If their approach had been more professional, I would have happily shared what Juliet had told me. I also wondered why Sue said the case had been shelved when clearly, it hadn't been. I had to give her a ring.

'Sue.'

'Yes, it's me. What do you want?' she said abruptly.

'I've just had two police officers from the Met on my doorstep.'

'Why?'

'They accused me of impersonating a police officer.'

'Were you?'

'No, of course not.'

'Then don't worry about it.'

‘If you don’t mind me saying, you sound slightly upset.’

‘That’s because I am.’

‘Why?’

‘You know why.’

‘Sorry, I don’t.’

‘I was suspended from duty this morning. There’s an internal investigation going on.’

‘What about?’

‘Virna bloody Babineaux. That’s what about. You’ve got me into some serious trouble, you have.’

‘Me? How? You’re the one who told me something was still worth pursuing even though the case had been dropped.’

‘Only the Surrey part of the investigation. We were only looking at the mysterious goings on at the house in Littlewick Road. But no, you had to go and do more digging, and now the Met think you are a person of interest. Thanks, or no thanks to you, my skipper thinks that I’m also implicated somehow.’

‘And that’s why you’ve been suspended?’

‘Of course, that’s why.’

‘Sorry.’

‘And so you should be.’

‘How long do you think you’ll be suspended for?’

‘Until I lose my job. That’s how long it usually takes.’

‘I’m sure it won’t come to that.’

‘It had better not. I need this job. I love this job and can’t imagine doing anything else. Now, fuck off!’

The day’s events had shaken me up, and I felt a quick walk to Sainsbury's in the rain to grab a bottle of something was necessary.

On the whole, my drinking habit had been more sporadic of late rather than daily. A small step in the right direction, which I felt at least was some progress.

I was about to settle down for the evening and watch some football when there was a familiar rattle on the front door.

‘Sue.’

‘Yes, Hun, it’s me,’ she said, pushing me to one side. ‘Here, I’ve brought you something to say sorry for earlier. I didn’t mean to tell you to fuck off. I’m sorry. It was the heat of the moment thing. Here, I'll help you drink it,' she said, pulling a litre bottle of Jameson's from her rucksack.'

'I've been over to Sainsbury's and got one myself. I've only just opened it.'

'Good. We'll drink both bottles then. Have you got any ice?'

'Yes, in the freezer. I'll get it.'

'Thanks.'

'I'm sorry you've been suspended.'

'Stop right there! I don't want to talk about it. I need a bit of company. Come on, let's watch and enjoy the football. Who's playing?'

'I can't remember.'

'Some football fan you are, then.'

After about twenty minutes, Sue had fallen asleep with her head on my shoulder. I took the empty glass out of her hand and moved to sit on the floor.

'Stay where you are. I need you where you are,' she said, opening her right eye.

Everything felt awkward. I knew I was drinking more than I should. By this time, Sue had fully woken and downed a couple more whiskies.

'Oops, time to go. I better not drive. Can you call me a taxi?'

'Taxi? It'll cost about twenty quid this time of the night. You know what robbing bastards they are round here.'

'Unless you want me to say the night?'

'Stay then. You know where the bedroom is. I'll kip down here on the sofa.'

'Oh no, you won't,' Sue said, grabbing my hand.

The next thing I knew, we were both upstairs, sitting on the bed. Sue was already naked whilst I refused to remove my boxer shorts.

'Come on, quickly, what's keeping you?' said Sue, with an air of anticipation.

'Sorry, nothing is going to happen. It'll all end badly as it did before.'

'Oh, Daniel, don't be such a bloody coward.'

'I'm being sensible, that's all.'

'No, you're not. You're just scared that the same thing will happen the last time we tried to make out.'

'What? That I didn't want to fuck you then either?'

'No, it was you and that bloody whiskey. When I go to bed, I expect to be with a man. A real man! Not some drunk who only cares about himself.'

'I am a real man. And I do care about other people!'

'Come on Danny Boy. Get to grips. The last time we slept together, it was like trying to force a marshmallow into a money box. You were so fucking pathetic.'

'That was when you had been telling me about your previous conquests. Hundreds of them. What a turn-off that was!'

'Now, you're exaggerating as well as making excuses.'

'Well, it's true. I want a proper girlfriend. Someone I can trust.'

'What, and love?'

'Well, yes!'

'Then you should never have been with me in the first place. I've always been honest and told you what I'm like.'

'I know, I know. I'm sorry.'

'Look, now you can make amends. Put it all behind you. Let me play with you a little bit, and when it gets hard, I'll let you push it into my little hole. Simple?'

'Sue. I don't want to have sex with you. I know I have things to prove to myself, but not with you. I'm happy for us to be just friends.'

'Friends, my ass.'

'Well, you're the one who's always asking if we're still friends. I don't want the benefits anymore. Not, after all I've been through.'

'There you go again, self, self, self. You ought not to flatter yourself either. And you wonder why I feel sorry for you? Just fuck off and join the masturbating millions. You don't need a woman in your life. You need you!'

'Oh, thanks for that. I'm quite capable of feeling sorry for myself. I don't want you looking after my emotions for me. Why do you have to behave like such a fucking whore?'

'Daniel. You can be such a cun…'

'Stop there. You're pissed!'

'Sorry, I didn't mean to use that word, but you had it coming.'

‘Please, please. Let’s leave it there. I don’t need this, and I’m sure you don’t!’

‘O Danny boy, the pipes, the pipes are calling
From glen to glen and down the mountainside
The summer’s gone, and all the roses falling
‘Tis you, ’tis you must go, and I must bide,’ sang Sue.

‘Oh, for fuck’s sake. Singing “Danny Boy” is one way of changing the subject, I suppose.’

‘Come on, Hun, fuck me. FUCK me!’

‘No chance. I know you have a lovely singing voice. My name’s Daniel, NOT Danny, anyway. Now, either sober up or get out!’

‘Ooh, touchy, touchy. Come on, okay, have it your way. Who fucking cares anyway?’

‘I do, actually!’

Sue’s demeanour suddenly changed.

‘Let’s get some sleep,’ she said. ‘I’ve got another shit day ahead of me tomorrow, and I need my wits about me.’

After Sue had left in the morning, all the self-analysis about moral standards began to hit me. Suggesting she could stay the night to avoid the taxi fare was a huge mistake. I knew I hadn’t done myself any favours.

19

The last few days, dare I say, had still been enjoyable. There were still a lot of things swirling around inside my head. Essentially, I was doing my best not to overthink things, especially when it came to Sue. Now, for once, for the first time in months, I was finally feeling optimistic about things, but I needed Sue out of my life, once and for all.

Sue had just sent me a Whatsapp message saying she was looking forward to returning to work after being told the charge against her had been rescinded. In fact, during her appeal, the Chief Constable praised her for engaging the press as she sought to solve the case. She doubted that I would hear from the Met anymore, which came as something of a relief. That said, I knew I shouldn't count my chickens.

Now, it was all about the next steps. Where and when to make my next move without attracting unwanted attention?

I kept thinking about Helena Cieslak, the Polish woman. Something in the back of my mind wasn't adding up. I had seen from the post-mortem report at the morgue that she was named as the person who had identified Virna's body just after the murder. I don't remember her mentioning that when I spoke to her a few weeks ago. She told me she was in Poland when Virna was killed, so how did she find out? I was a little confused. I felt the need to travel to London and speak to Helena again to clarify things.

On arrival at Waterloo, I decided to walk down to Lower Marsh, a street along the station's south side. There was a busy street-food market, and all the lunchtime office workers were out with their nose-bags on. I found the sex shop, Honour, where Virna's neighbour, Alwyn Peters, had been photographed. There were a couple of mannequins in the window. The way they were dressed told me enough about the place, so I decided not to go in. Just as I was about to walk away, the shop door opened, and a woman was trying to wave me in.

'No, it's alright. I was only looking at the window display,' I said.

As she stepped out onto the pavement, I thought I recognised her.

'We know each other, don't we?' she said as she started to roll a cigarette. 'I'm Helena.'

'Helena from the pub?'

'Yes, except that I don't work there anymore.'

'Flipping heck. I've actually come up to London to speak to you. The Ring was my next port of call.'

'I left there three weeks ago. There was a vacancy here. Patrice, an old friend, owns the shop and asked if I could come and help.'

'So, you said yes.'

'I did. Anyway, I wasn't enjoying working at the pub too much. The landlord had it in for me. There were always people like the police coming into the place and asking questions. He was giving me a hard time, always saying that I was disgracing the establishment and that he wished he had never employed me. Luckily, Mara, one of the other barmaids, always stuck up for me, so he backed off.'

'I see. Are you happier now?'

'Yes, very much so. Look, I've got an hour for lunch. There's a quiet Chinese café further along. I was popping out for something to eat. At least we can get out of the rain. I suspect you want to talk about Virna again, don't you?'

'If you don't mind.'

'Well, put it this way, I do, and I don't.'

Once inside the café, Helena ordered sweet and sour pork balls with plain rice. I had the duck in black bean sauce.

'Come on then. Why do you want to speak to me?'

'Of course, you're right. It is about Virna. I want to clear some things up, that's all.'

'What things?'

'Firstly, did you ever meet the artist, Jonathan Blackwell?'

'I knew of him but never met him. Virna was besotted by him and absolutely loved his paintings. She once told me she had a large collection of his work.'

'Yes, I know, I've seen it. Do you know anything about an altercation between Jonathan Blackwell and Robert Surcouf?'

'I heard there was a fight. Surcouf was a very jealous and violent man. He wouldn't have liked another man going with Virna.'

'Even though she was a prostitute?'

'That was different. Surcouf thought he owned her. He always said he loved her. He didn't. It was obvious to everyone it was Virna's money he loved. That was the kind of man he was!'

'You said you were in Poland staying with relatives when Virna was killed.'

'That's right. I was.'

'Who told you she had been murdered?'

'I found out when I returned a couple of days later. There was blue and white police tape all over my front door and a note in a small plastic bag stuck to the knocker with my name on it. When I opened it, there was a policeman's contact name and number. My mobile phone was dead after all the travelling back from Poland. I rushed across the road to my friend Trudi's house. Trudi opened the door and thrust her arms around me. It was then I knew something was terribly wrong. "There's been a murder, there's been a murder," she kept saying. I remember the poor girl sobbing uncontrollably. It took a long time for her to stop. When I asked her who had been murdered, she didn't know.'

'How come?'

'It could have been any one of three or four girls. They worked in shifts and didn't keep to any particular working patterns. For all I knew, it could have even been a punter. Maybe one of the girls overreacted when she was defending herself. I didn't know. All sorts of things were going through my mind.'

'Did you call the police number?'

'Yes. It took about two hours. Trudi was very kind. She said I could stay in her spare room for a few nights until I sorted myself out. I was there for eighteen months in the end. When the police let me access my house, I didn't want to go back except to collect a few things. There was still blood all over the walls and floor. It was horrible. I sold the property to an Italian family for only half the market price. That's when I got my flat around the corner in Hatfields. I needed to get rid of the house. I see it's being renovated now.'

'Yes, I've seen the workmen and all the scaffolding.'

'You know where the house is?'

'I found out that day when I last spoke to you. I had been in the Kings Arms, and an old guy called Alf told me. It did cost me a couple of pints, though.'

'Old Alf? Everyone knows him. He comes across as a sweet old man. He wanders around all the pubs and loves to tell old stories about this part of London. He also likes to gossip, so I don't trust him.'

'Oh. I see. Anyway, I understand you had to identify Virna's body.'

'How do you know that?'

'I've seen your name on the original post-mortem report.'

'Oh!'

'I visited the West London Morgue and spoke to the senior forensic pathologist. Did you know Virna's body was there?'

'No. At first, I knew there hadn't been a funeral. However, I did wonder if Virna had later been buried in secret. I was angry I wasn't told but realised no-one knew me anyway.'

'I need to tell you. There never was a funeral. In fact, Virna's body has gone missing from the morgue.'

'What? As in stolen?'

'Possibly, yes.'

'I don't understand.'

'Don't worry. Nor do I, but that's what I'm trying to get to the bottom of.'

'Poor Virna.'

'Poor Virna indeed. Can I ask? Who asked you to identify the body?'

'It was a police sergeant. He came to see me at Trudi's house and said there were no known relatives they could contact. It was two or three weeks after Virna had been killed. I said no, at first, but he pleaded with me and said I would only make things worse for myself. He kept reminding me that I should be responsible as Virna had died in my house. You know, duty. That kind of thing. In the end, I felt obliged so reluctantly agreed.'

'Did they take you to West London Morgue?'

'No. The sergeant and a very nice policewoman took me to a mortuary at a hospital near Wimbledon.'

'Wimbledon?'

'Yes, I think so. A place called St George's.'

'I think that's in Tooting, but I know where you mean.'

'I stood behind a glass window, and they pulled the shroud from Virna's face. I could hardly look. Her face was ashen, you know, a grey colour. They had tried to hide all the bruises and scratches with makeup. Her hair seemed shorter; it wasn't the Virna I knew. She looked so different, but then I suppose dead people do. Don't forget, it was a long time after she had been killed, and the mortuary lady told me what to expect.'

'So, were you sure it was Virna's body?'

'As sure as I could be. It was a horrible experience. I just wanted to get out of there. The police sergeant was going to give me a lift back to Trudi's house, but I made an excuse that I would like to do some shopping, and he dropped me off outside Ely's department store in Wimbledon.'

'So, you went shopping?'

'No, I found a pub called the Alexandra and got myself a large vodka. Straight, nothing in it. I drank it down and then bought another and then another. Two very nice young boys in their twenties sat at my table and bought me more. I never did find out how I got back to Trudi's house that night.'

Time was getting on, and I knew Helena had to return to work.

'The other girls who worked with Virna at your house. What were their names?'

'There was Emma, Gina and Tina. Virna was the only one who used her own name.'

'What do you mean?'

'None of the girls would want the punters to know their real names. Personal safety and security and all that. Most working girls use an alias.'

'But Virna didn't?'

'Virna still regarded herself as a high-class glamour model. She was so obsessed with her reputation. She knew that by keeping her name, she could demand higher fees from her clients, and in most cases, she got them.'

'What sort of fees?'

'Put it this way. The other girls would get £50 a trick, up to £100 if they were lucky. Virna would regularly command a fee of between £1,000 and £5,000. That's why that asshole, Surcouf, came back out of the woodwork and tried to kill her.'

'Tried?'

'Sorry. I mean, he did, didn't he?'

Helena began packing things into her handbag, and I offered to pay the bill. Both of us had hardly touched our food because of all the talking. We left the café and wandered back on to the street outside towards her shop. It had stopped raining, and the sun was starting to come out. As Helena reached for the key to the shop door, I thanked her for her time. Surprisingly, she gave me a peck on the cheek and told me to be careful. I wasn't sure why.

Before catching a train back to Woking, I decided to take another walk along Roupell Street. I wondered about Helena's friend Trudi and decided to look her up. Across the road from Helena's old house were a couple of blocks of flats belonging to the Peabody Trust. There was a large security gate, so entry was nigh on impossible. I had forgotten to ask Helena for Trudi's surname, which didn't help, so I was feeling quite angry with myself.

'Are you alright, dear?' Asked an old lady who was walking a small black dog.

'Yes, fine. Thank you. That's a nice pup you have there.'

'This is Stella. Say "Hello", Stella.' The dog looked up at me, somewhat puzzled by my sudden attention.

'What breed is she?'

'I was told she's a cross between a Patterdale terrier and a Jack Russell. The father was the Patterdale.'

'Can I take her home with me?' I joked.

'No, you can't,' she laughed.

'Anyway, I was wondering if you could help me. I was looking for someone called Trudi who lives around here. She's a friend of a friend.'

'There's only one Trudi that I know of. She used to live over there,' said the old lady pointing to a house with railings.

'Oh, great, thank you.'

'She's not there anymore. She died.'

'Died?'

'Yes, a couple of years ago from that dreadful Covid thing. Such a shame. She had a heart of gold. She would help anyone.'

'Thank you. I think I know.'

'You're very welcome young man.'

'Just one other thing. Do you know someone called Helena Cieslak who used to live in the house with all the scaffolding up?'

'That whore! Don't speak to me about her,' she said. 'That woman brought great shame on this street with all her shenanigans. Did you know there was a murder in that house?'

'Yes, I did.'

'I never understood why Trudi wanted to help her. But as I said, poor Trudi had a heart of gold. She didn't deserve to die so young!'

'How old was she?'

'Only in her forties. I'm ninety-two, you know.'

'I do now. Thank you.'

After popping into the Kings Arms for a quick pint, I caught a train back to Woking, which gave me plenty of time to think.

I had now convinced myself that Helena wasn't telling the truth. And why, at the end of the conversation, did Helena say that Robert Surcouf had only tried to kill Virna? Things didn't quite add up. She knew a whole lot more than what she was telling me.

20

It had been a couple of weeks since I had spoken to Helena, and I was beginning to get quite anxious as not much else had been happening. I had submitted other articles to a couple of magazines, but that was it. I needed to keep the bread-and-butter stuff going. After all, I was still struggling to pay my bills.

I had been laying off the whiskey lately, so I felt quite pleased with myself. A beer or two wouldn't hurt. Besides, I still needed a social life to meet and catch up with my friends. I decided to walk around the corner for a quick pint at the Garibaldi.

The pub was fairly quiet at first, so I was able to exchange pleasantries with Jack, the barman, mostly about football and England's chances in the World Cup. I thought I was pessimistic, but he was even more critical and made it clear he was a rugby fan.

'Football ain't my thing,' he said. 'They'll all be coming home empty-handed soon, mark my word. 'I'm not usually a betting man, but I've got a ton on Argentina to win anyway,' he laughed.

I found a high table by the door, watched the traffic from the window, and stared down at my phone.

'Oh, crikey, Marianne, look who's here.'

I looked up. It was one of my old neighbours, Eddie Noble, and his beautiful new wife, who had recently moved from Knaphill to Camberley.

'Flipping heck, Eddie. I didn't think I'd see you in here again.'

'Camberley's not too far away. Anyway, we've just been over to see one of Marianne's old friends and thought we'd pop in for lunch.'

'Good. It's great to see you and finally meet Marianne properly,' I said, smiling in her direction.

'Oh, sorry, this is Marianne, the love of my life.'

'Pleased to meet you, Marianne.'

'Likewise,' she said.

'So, Daniel, what have you been up to lately? Are you still shagging that copper? What's her name, Sue?'

‘That’s one way of putting it, but the answer is no, well, not really.’

‘What do you mean, not really?’

‘Put it this way. We’re still friends.’

‘Ah, got it—a friend with benefits,’ he said, winking at Marianne. ‘Look, we’re going to sit down and eat over in the corner. Would you like to join us?’

‘No, but thanks for your kind offer, though. I’m just going to have another quick pint, and then I’m off.’

‘Are you sure? You’re more than welcome.’

‘I’m sure, positive thanks. Things to do and all that!’

‘Okay, make sure to take care of yourself!’

‘I will. You take care as well and look after that pretty wife of yours.’

Marianne turned and smiled. ‘Thank you,’ she said.

I was about to leave the pub when a guy called Joe walked in. He’s a retired postman and knows all the local gossip.

‘Are you staying?’ he asked.

‘I might now,’ I said. ‘I must owe you a couple of pints after all these years.’

‘Damn right you do, lad, damn right you do. Is it alright if I join you?’

‘Of course.’

Joe was always an excellent source for any local story when I was at the Tribune. He was a well-known police informer and had a few enemies. He was never frightened to tip me off if something juicy happened. A valuable person to know for anyone in the reporting game.

‘How have you been, lad? I haven’t seen you for months.’

‘That’s because I’ve left the Tribune. I’m working for myself now.’

‘What? As a freelancer?’

‘Yes, all setup and ready to make the big bucks.’

‘You’re joking?’

‘Unfortunately, I am. I couldn’t stay at the Tribune any longer. It had become a right old shit show. It was unbearable.’

‘I thought something was up. A little bird tells me the editor was sacked a couple of weeks ago.’

‘Who? Tom Challis?’

'Yes, that's him. Word has it Challis was printing fake news.'

'Flipping heck, although that doesn't surprise me. That man is a complete asshole!'

'Did you know the Tribune was on the verge of being taken to court?'

'No, I didn't. I have no real interest in the paper these days.'

'Something to do with the council. Anyhow, all the charges against the paper got scrapped.'

'The council is corrupt as well. I've heard it's got some mounting debts that could see them go bust. It sounds like all the backhanders are still happening, despite all the changes at the top,' I said as I signalled for more drinks to Jack behind the bar.

'No doubt they are. Well, I know they are. I still like to keep my nose to the ground,' said Joe.

'Obviously.'

'Oh, by the way, did you know there was a suicide in Littlewick Road yesterday?'

'No, shit, I didn't. Whereabouts?'

'One of the posh houses. Next door to where that prostitute used to live. You know, the one who got murdered in London a few years back.'

'Virna Babineaux.'

'Yes, that's her. Bloody hell, lad, you have a good memory.'

'It's all about a story I'm still working on. Hopefully, it might help me make those big bucks I was talking about.'

'You jest!'

'I do, I do. Going back to what you've just told me, do you know who committed suicide? I know the neighbours on both sides of where Virna used to live.'

'I know it was a male. Yesterday afternoon, I saw all the police activity while cycling up to the Royal Oak. There were three police cars and one of those black private ambulances.'

'How do you know it was a male?'

'You know me, the police know me, so I stopped and asked. The young constable told me. He said a woman had found her husband hanging from a beam at the top of the stairs. The funny thing was a bright red Toyota Yaris pulled up in the driveway, and a woman sitting in a wheelchair got up and ran towards it like an athlete. I saw it with my own eyes.'

'Who was driving?'

'It was another woman from what I could make out. The young constable removed his cap and scratched his head. All very bizarre it was.'

'I think the woman must be Lucy Peters. She's been disabled since a horse-riding accident. That must have been Alwyn, her husband, who had killed himself.'

'So, you know them, lad?'

'Yes, of course.'

'I remember the name Peters from when I was still a postman. That house had been in the family for donkey's years.'

'Yes, I know,' I said, looking at the time.

'I remember that Alywn chappy. He was a bit queer you know. People were more than surprised when he got wed, and they say it wasn't his first time either.'

'What?'

'He was married twice before.'

'Despite being gay? I don't believe it.'

'They say it was to cover up the fact that he was queer. Bisexual, he used to call himself.'

'Well, don't repeat this. I know Alwyn liked to swing both ways and was heavily into bondage. I've seen the proof,' I said.

'Go on, lad, pray, tell me more.'

'No, best if I don't. I've told you enough already.'

'I won't go running off to the Tribune with it if that's what you're worried about,' chuckled Joe.

'Let me say, if I see it printed in the Tribune, I shall know where they got it from.'

'Christ, lad, you know me too well.'

I bought Joe another pint and finally decided to leave, waving to Eddie and Marianne as I went. My quick pint had rapidly turned into five, and I felt a little light-headed. I now wondered why Alwyn had taken his own life, although I knew I had to verify the story through a second channel before pursuing anything. Perhaps Sue might know?

I tried to ring, but the phone kept going to voicemail, so I asked her to call me back when she could.

Joe claimed he witnessed Lucy jumping out of her wheelchair and running over to a car which puzzled me. She can't be as disabled as she's been making out.

21

A rare text message from Bill Pattenden asking me if I would be at home this morning surprised me. 'Yes,' I answered, then heard nothing more until the doorbell rang a couple of hours later.

'Bill!'

'Wotcha, matey. Put the kettle on. I'm parched.'

'What can I do for you besides a cup of tea?'

'Nothing. It's more about what you can do for yourself.'

'Sorry, I don't know what you mean?'

'Procrastination. That's what I mean!'

'In what sense?' I asked.

'In dragging your heels, being a lazy bugger. Waiting for things to come to you. That's what I mean.'

'Excuse me?'

'How long have you been working on your Babineaux story now?'

'Since September. Around the time the Queen died. Why?'

'Why? You don't need to ask me fucking "Why?" For heaven's sake, Blue Boy. You should have had it all sewn up and in the bag by now.'

'Well, it's taking me longer than I thought it would.'

'That's because you've been sat on your fat backside doing nothing. Good stories don't just come to you. You need to go out and grab them. Do the fucking footwork. Do you get my fucking drift?'

'Sorry, Bill. You sound angry. Anyway, I have done some footwork. I've been to London a few times and spoken to people.'

'What, talking to old ladies out walking their dogs? For fuck sake, you were doing that when we were at the Chronicle. You have to speak to real people. The people who are actually involved in the story you are investigating.'

'I have been speaking to real people.'

'Who?'

'Helena Cieslak, She's the woman who acted as a maid around the time Virna was murdered.'

'Who else?'

'The senior forensic pathologist at the West London Morgue. Virna's former neighbours in Littlewick Road, Iona Turner and Alywn Peters. Oh, and Alwyn recently killed himself. Did you know?'

'I didn't, but do you understand what I'm trying to say?'

'Sort of.'

'There's no bloody sort of about it. You should have all the answers by now. Do you know what happened to Babineaux's body?'

'No.'

'Do you know the current whereabouts of Jonathan Blackwell?'

'No.'

'Do you know who attacked Iona Turner?'

'No, but I have my suspicions.'

'Not good enough. Now, do you see where I'm coming from?'

'I think so.'

'Think so? You should fucking know so! Any investigative journalist worth their salt would have been on to their next story by now. You remind me of a freelance called Addison-Jones. What a complete lazy-ass bastard he was. He thought he knew everything but knew nothing. On top of that, he was fucking useless. The last time I heard, he was pulling pints in a Spanish tapas bar in Barcelona. You, Blue Boy, have much more potential, and that's why I'm here.'

'Sorry, I do tend to trip myself up sometimes.'

'Drink?'

'Sometimes, but not so much these days.'

'Women?'

'Ha, ha. Sore point.'

'Look. Talking of women, the old girl walked out on me a couple of weeks ago. It's a bit lonely. A bit tough. You must know what I mean?'

'Of course I do.'

'It's given me plenty of time to look into things, including your Babineaux story. I remember some of the things Anouska, I mean Annie, had been looking at. Is it right that you've been to Portland and now the Isle of Wight, looking for the artist fellow?'

‘Yes. I found out Jonathan left his wife in Freshwater after a French woman came looking for him. I was told he ran off with her.’

‘Have you considered who this French woman might have been?’

‘No. Should I have done?’

‘Too fucking right, you should have.’

‘Why?’

‘What if it was Virna Babineaux?’

‘She’s dead.’

‘Come on, Blue Boy, look outside the box. What if she’s not?’

‘Well, there may have been a mix-up at the morgue, and the wrong body was taken away by undertakers at some point.’

‘That’s not where I’m coming from. What if Babineaux was never in the morgue? What if it was someone else?’

‘Come to think of it, as you say. It might not have been.’

‘Explain.’

‘When I spoke to Helena Cieslak the other week, we discussed identifying Virna’s body. Helena’s name was on the post-mortem document I had seen when I visited the morgue. I’ve spoken to Helena twice now. The first time I saw her, she didn’t even mention the fact it was her who identified the body.’

‘Go on.’

‘Well, to be honest, I had forgotten to ask Helena the first time I met her. That’s precisely why I went back a second time. I needed to find out more.’

‘And?’

‘When I asked her about the day she identified Virna, she came over as a little coy. Reluctant, you know what I mean. I guess she didn’t want to answer the question. It became clear to me that she didn’t view the body properly. She admitted telling the police it was Virna without being fully sure. I was going to mention it to someone, but I still hadn’t decided who.’

‘Procrastination again. And now you’ve told me. In your heart of hearts, where do you think your story is going?’

‘I think I’m getting close to a resolution, but not close enough.’

‘You must take those blinkers off and look outside the box. What does the name Robert Surcouf mean to you?’

‘He’s the guy who was convicted alongside William Kuznia for Virna’s murder. Surcouf wasn’t his real name, though,’ I said.

‘Yes, Blue Boy, I know. I’ve recently read up on all that as well.’

‘Excuse me. Can I ask a quick question? Have you been speaking to Annie about all this?’

‘If I’m honest, yes. Metaphorically speaking, we’ve had a frank and meaningful conversation and made up. We’ve spoken a lot lately. She always seems one step ahead of the game, which is exactly where you should be!’

‘Yeah, sorry. I get it.’

‘Never say sorry. It’s a sign of weakness.

‘Even if I’m wrong?’

‘More so,’ said Bill, scrutinising his empty coffee mug.

‘Mm.’

‘Now, St Malo, France. Does that mean anything to you?’

‘Yes, of course. It’s where the original Robert Surcouf was born.’

‘Good. So, you’ve been looking at Wikipedia as well?’

‘Would you like another cup of tea?’ I asked, hoping Bill would calm down.

‘No thanks. It’s past noon now. Have you got anything stronger? I know you like the whiskey.’

‘Actually, I haven’t. I’m trying to keep off the stuff. Besides, you’re driving anyway.’

‘Fair point, Now, you would have noticed I’ve brought my tablet. There are a couple of pictures I want you to look at. Here’s the first...’

‘It’s a statue.’

‘Do you know who it is?’

‘No,’ I said curiously.

‘It’s Robert Surcouf, 12 December 1773 – 8 July 1827.’

‘Yes, I’ve seen those dates before.’

‘The statue is on the beach in St Malo.’

‘Look, here’s another picture with the same statue in the background.’

‘Artists.’

‘Yes, displaying their work on the beach.’

‘And here’s another.’

‘Is that who I think it is?’

‘Yes, the artist you are trying to track down. One Jonathan Blackwell.’

‘Flipping heck. That’s a co-incidence. Blackwell and the Surcouf statue, I mean.’

‘And there’s more. Wait!’

Bill began frantically scrolling through the website he was showing me, but then everything froze.

‘Fuck it. It would be best if you saw these last couple of pictures. Ah, here we go, take a look.’

‘It’s Jonathan Blackwell with a woman.’

‘Ah, but what woman? Take a closer look,’ said Bill excitedly.

‘I can’t see anything obvious.’

‘Then take a look at this one.’

‘Fucking hell. Do you think that is Virna Babineaux?’ I asked.

‘I’m almost certain. What do you think?’

‘Now I’ve seen the close-up of her face. I’m almost convinced, but not one hundred per cent.’

‘These pictures were taken at an art fayre in St Malo in August. The website states all the work displayed is by Brittany-based artists. I have a hunch that Jonathan Blackwell and your Babineaux lady if it is her, are living in that vicinity.’

‘I guess I need to start an internet search to try and find an address.’

‘No, don’t. That’ll be a waste of time. Nothing would show up if the pair had only been living there recently. Besides, Annie has already had a look for me. You need to get over to France and ask a few questions. Do you speak any French?’

‘Err, no,’

‘I didn’t think so. Fortunately, Annie can.’

‘She’s prepared to go over there with you. You can get a ferry to St Malo from Portsmouth. Let me know when you want to go, and I’ll book it. You’ll need to give Annie a call. She’ll be expecting to hear from you. Make sure you get over there before Christmas. You, Blue Boy, have wasted enough time on this already. I’ll be paying for two nights for your trip and hotel bill, so I want value for my money.’

‘Two nights?’

‘Yes, any more than that, then you’re paying,’ Bill laughed.
‘Thanks. No pressure then.’
‘No pressure at all. Just don’t let me down.’
‘I won’t.’
After Bill left, I felt I had been pushed headfirst through a mangle. He gave me such a roasting. I had never been bollocked like that before. He made me feel I was still a kid working back at the Chronicle.
The thought that Virna could still be alive had crossed my mind, but I had never considered it a real possibility. Before I rang Annie, I thought I’d go back through everything I had on the story just in case there was anything else I may have missed.

22

I had meant to attend Alwyn Peters' funeral at Woking Crematorium yesterday, but one thing led to another, and time got the better of me. I wasn't sure if it would have been to my benefit anyway. As Bill said, I needed to get the story written and in the bag. All the goings on in Littlewick Road had been holding me back.

I tried calling Annie about arranging our trip to France, but her phone kept going to voicemail, and she wasn't replying to my messages.

Worryingly, I still hadn't been able to get hold of Sue, but I did bump into one of her colleagues, the aptly named Denise Copper, who said Sue was on holiday in Venice. Denise used to be called Smithers, and then she married a plumber named Kevin Copper a few years ago. Sue once told me it caused a big commotion at the police station as all the other officers were taking the piss. Apparently, Denise coped with it by even taking the piss out of herself. I was now wondering who Sue had gone to Venice with. No doubt another poor unsuspecting sod, I thought.

I needed to pop into Woking and look for a new pair of walking boots. The weather was on the turn, and I realised I had no suitable footwear. I decided to take my Harley out for a rare spin. It may be my last chance, as I know I will probably have to sell the thing unless my financial situation vastly improves within the next few weeks.

I was standing on an escalator after coming out of Marks and Spencer's in Victoria Place when I felt a tap on my shoulder.

'Hello. Remember me?' said a female voice.

I waited a split second until I reached the bottom, then turned round.

'Oh, Hello!' I said, somewhat startled. It was Lucy Peters.

'You're that journalist guy, aren't you?'

'Indeed, I am a journalist. I was sorry to hear about your loss. I had planned to come to Alwyn's funeral yesterday, but things got in the way. I'm so sorry.'

'Don't be. Anyway, have you got time to go somewhere quiet and talk?'

'Of course. I've only come into town to buy some boots. So long as I don't forget to do that, it's fine.'

'Good. I have some things to tell you.'

'I don't doubt it,' I said, remembering what old Joe had told me in the Garibaldi when I saw him.

Lucy was insistent that we go to Luciano's, an Italian restaurant and bar on Commercial Way.

'It's one of my favourite places on earth now. The food is gorgeous, the prices are reasonable, and the staff are lovely,' she said.

'Okay, we'll go there, then,' I said, not knowing what would happen next.

'Don't worry. I'll pay. My treat. Besides, I could do with an intelligent conversation.'

I just laughed.

'Here, this is my favourite spot. It's a great place to people-watch, don't you think?'

'If you say so.'

'Take a look at the menu. I can fully recommend the sea bass.'

'Thank you. Oh, if you don't mind me asking. The last time I saw you, you were in a wheelchair. I'm assuming you've fully recovered now?'

'To be honest, the chair was a prop. It was my way of fooling Alwyn into thinking I was still an invalid. Yes, I had a horse-riding accident and badly damaged my back. It healed after about six months. I played on it, that's all.'

'Why?'

'Over the last few years, I had known Alwyn was up to all sorts of things. With me being in a wheelchair, it gave him a false sense of security.'

'How?'

'He thought I was immobilised. He didn't realise I was following him into the house next door and watching everything he was up to.'

'Are you talking about Iona Turner?'

‘Not just that old witch. He was taking men up there as well. What I saw him doing was disgusting. He was a bit of a poof, you know.’

‘I did. Alwyn once confided in me that he thought you went to Bingo on Wednesday nights, and that’s when he went in there with Iona.’

‘He did, did he?’

‘Well, that’s what he told me.’

‘He was going in there at all times of the day. He would always meet people around the back. They would enter the house through a tunnel that goes into the cellar.’

‘Yes, I know, I’ve seen it.’

‘He was always trying to be very quiet, but I got used to his movements. It was always the same few people he saw in there.’

‘How did you watch what was going on without him realising?’

‘When Virna Babineaux was alive, she had a CCTV camera installed. It was linked up to a recorder in the front downstairs room. The recorder was hidden in a chestnut bureau in the corner. It was easy to watch. I always took my earplugs so I could listen discreetly.’

‘Flipping heck. I thought it was only Iona he saw in there.’

‘To the contrary, as I said, most of the others were mainly men. There were a couple of women, one quite old and one much younger. In fact, I recognised her.’

‘Who?’

‘That detective inspector woman, what’s her name? She was the one who had the audacity to come round and ask us questions about certain goings on in the house, and again when Iona was attacked.’

‘DI Sue Grendel?’

‘Yes, that’s her. How could she? A policewoman as well, she certainly should know better. That upset me.’

‘Fucking hell. I’m not surprised. Sorry, I didn’t mean to swear. What you’ve told me is all a bit of a shock.’

‘Alwyn never wanted to touch me. He always said I was too frigid. I always knew he liked men and thought I could change him. Rather naïve of me, don’t you think?’

‘Perhaps.’

‘Look, I can tell you, but please don’t repeat this to a soul!’

‘What?’

‘I haven’t had sex for over ten years, and it’s beginning to hurt. Alwyn held me back. After seeing what he was doing, it repulsed me. I didn’t want him near me. Towards the end, I told him to fuck off, but he didn’t. He just stood there, grinned, and called me an ungrateful little cabbage. Little did he know.’

‘Little did he know you were strong and healthy?’

‘Exactly. The day after, I plucked up the courage to stand up and tell him everything. I stepped out of my wheelchair, did a little jig and slapped him around the face. The sad, twisted bastard fell to his knees, crying. The next morning, I found him hanging over the stairs.’

‘And you are telling me all this the day after his funeral?’

‘The crematorium was full of sycophants and weirdos. I just sat there, hiding my face behind a veil. I felt so ashamed I couldn’t speak. People were glaring at me. I know they were blaming me for Alwyn’s death. It was so uncomfortable. The vicar was stuttering on all his words. At one point, he had to pause for a glass of water. Afterwards, outside, it was chaos. Most of the flower arrangements were rainbow colours. Almost everyone there was referring to Alwyn as kind-hearted, generous and the life and soul of the party. It was unnerving. They didn’t know him as a cruel, callous, calculating pervert as I did.’

‘I’m sorry.’

‘You don’t need to be. Even I know there is a fragile line between extreme sex and what some might call perversion. There must be many occasions when the grey areas cross over each other. It’s not my kind of thing. That’s all!’

‘Not mine, either. Let me say the jury is still out on that one.’

‘Have you got a wife or girlfriend?’

‘Not anymore. If I did have, I certainly wouldn’t after this conversation.’

‘Sorry, I don’t understand.’

‘You mentioned DI Sue Grendel earlier.’

‘I did, yes. What about her?’

‘Up until the summer, we had lived with each other for a while. I was fascinated with her, obsessed, even. Looking back, definitely not one of my greatest moves.’

'Oh!'

'Anyway, I went through a minor change of life thing. It was like a mini-breakdown, and I ended up drinking too much. Sue used it as an excuse to go out and find other men. I knew she was promiscuous when I first met her. It was part of my obsession. How sad is that?'

'It's not sad. We're all different. You only have to look at my situation.'

'Thank you. At least you seem to understand,' I said while checking the time.

'Of course, I understand. Now, Daniel, it is Daniel. Isn't it?'

'Yes, sorry. I should have confirmed that earlier.'

'I'm only teasing. I hope you've enjoyed the meal?'

'I have, thank you, despite all the talking.'

'Then you can reciprocate another time. Let's let things settle down a little first. I still have to play the grieving widow, you know. At least for the time being.'

'Yes, I get that.'

When we left the restaurant, Lucy went to the car park, and I went back into the shopping centre to search for a decent pair of boots.

I then noticed two missed calls on my mobile phone and a Whatsapp message from Annie.

'Sorry I missed your calls. I've been busy. I've spoken to Bill, and he's booking St Malo for us, a ferry and two nights from Friday 16 December. Please call me asap.'

Flipping heck. Not what I wanted, and the day before my birthday as well.

I called back.

'Daniel.'

'Hiya, yes, it's me. I've just seen your message.'

'Are you okay with those dates?'

'Yes, I suppose I'll have to be.'

'Good, I'll tell Bill. I think he will drive us to Portsmouth to ensure we get the ferry.'

'That's nice of him.'

'I did hear you've been in his bad books lately, my lovely.'

'You can say that again. I've never had such a bollocking.'

'Yes, he can get feisty when something rattles him.'

'Especially procrastination, I believe.'

'Yes, especially that. Look, I've got to go. See you soon. Take care.'

'I will, thanks.'

Having been to Annie's house, I think I know what she means by being busy. Let's leave it there, I thought.

23

It was a cold Saturday morning. Bill came to pick me up just as it was getting light. Annie was already in his car, which led me to believe she had spent the night at his place.

'Wotcha. Have you got everything you need?' he asked.

'Yes, I think so. Passport, toiletries, a change of underwear, if that's what you mean.'

'Good,' said Annie, 'I like my men to be clean.'

Bill laughed. 'Hearing that coming from you is priceless,' he said.

'Anyway, what time is our ferry?' I asked, interrupting to change the subject.

'20.15,' said Bill.

'20.15? That's nearly twelve hours away,' I gasped.

'Indeed, it is. We have a little surprise for you first,' said Annie.

'What?'

'Happy birthday to you, happy birthday to you.'

'Ah!' I murmured.

'I've forgotten, how old?' asked Annie.

'Forty-six. I feel like an old man in a young man's body, though.'

'You don't look it,' she said.

'That's very nice of you to say. I don't get many compliments these days.'

'You should. You are a very good-looking and sexy man,' said Annie.

'Oh my God,' said Bill. 'I can see in the rear-view mirror. Blue Boy's head is swelling up.'

We all laughed.

'So, what's this surprise?' I asked.

'Don't worry, it's nothing sordid or anything like that,' said Annie. 'Bill has recently bought a new house in Petersfield. It has an indoor pool and everything, doesn't it, Bill?'

'Yes, it does. It cost a fair few quid. It used to be in my family up until about thirty years ago. I was distraught when my old man decided to sell up. I always told my mother I would repurchase it, but she popped her clogs years ago. Now, I have it. The house has five bedrooms and a swimming pool. The pool is quite a new addition. The garden is massive. It has woodland at the bottom and a small stream. I have many fond memories of the old place. I just had to buy it when I saw it on the market.'

'And Bill is taking us there for dinner. We can have a swim, a few drinks and relax before getting the ferry,' said Annie.

'Consider it a small birthday treat. I've hired a Michelin star chef called Sarah to cook for us. She used to run a pub near you. She's been on the telly and everything. You may recognise her,' said Bill excitedly.

'That's very kind. Thank you.'

'There's a method in my madness. I want to talk to you both about the case before dumping you on the ferry. We can't afford any more fuck ups. That's why I've asked Annie to go with you.'

'Yes, I'll keep you on an even keel,' she said. 'See, Bill is rich and generous after all.'

'I don't know about that, but time is of the essence,' said Bill. 'I suggest you look for the artist guy first. It seems his paintings are quite popular in the area. Someone will know where he lives. Please don't ask questions about Babineaux until you're both sure you know where she is. Oh, and for fuck's sake, make sure it's her.'

'That was her in the photograph you showed me the other day, though, wasn't it?' I said.

'I think it is, but it's better to be safe than sorry. Remember, a lot of time has passed since she was supposedly murdered. People change. I think it is her. Just be careful that you don't jump to any conclusions, that's all.'

'In a way, you have. You both have already,' said Annie.

'Perhaps,' said Bill. 'Remember, we have the proof that Jonathan Blackwell is living in or around St Malo. The bottom line is, you find him, and you'll get what you're looking for.'

'I hope so,' I said.

'I don't want you coming back empty-handed. Besides, if you get it right and get me the full story before Christmas, I've secured an outlet for you,' said Bill, as he slowed the car down and turned left off the main road.

'Outlet? What kind of outlet?' I asked.

'You'll see. Just get me the story first.'

Already, Bill was driving us into the gravel driveway of his new home. Annie had nearly fallen asleep in the front passenger seat, and I was still annoyed because we had so much time to kill before going to Portsmouth to catch the ferry.

'Come on,' said Bill as he opened the front door. 'Oh, this is Sarah, our cook for the day,' Bill said as a young woman excitedly opened the front door.

'Chef, Bill. Chef, if you don't mind,' she joked.

Sarah was a very pretty woman in her early thirties. Slim with her straight brown hair tied back in a ponytail. She told us that she was half English and half Mauritian and that her estranged husband, Adonis, was hoping to buy a gastro pub near Brighton in an attempt to woo her back.

'Bill has asked me here to cook for your birthday, Daniel,' she said.

'Thank you.'

'We have a squid starter with asparagus and chillies. A duck main and a fantastic cheeseboard to compliment it all afterwards.'

'And plenty of wine to wash it down,' said Bill.

'But you'll be driving later,' said Annie.

'No, he won't. I'll be taking you both to Portsmouth. I've got to go that way later, anyway,' said Sarah.

'Oh, thank you so much, thank you,' said Annie as she gave Sarah a hug.

'Before I forget, here are the tickets,' said Bill, forcing them into my hand.

'Thank you. Thanks very much for all this,' I said.

'Results, Blue Boy. Now, get on and enjoy your day.'

I realised I had no swimming shorts, so I jumped into the pool, still wearing my boxers. Annie was more prepared as she walked around the pool in a red bikini with a white blouse over her shoulders. Bill kept walking in and out of the pool area with a large glass of his favourite red Italian merlot. He seemed happy talking with Sarah, and I wondered if there was more to it than met the eye. The next thing I knew, Annie dived into the pool naked.

'You like what you see?' she asked as she surfaced beside me.

'Well, I wasn't expecting that.'

'Call it a birthday surprise,' she said, kissing me on the cheek.

'Thank you.'

'There's no need to thank me,' she whispered, grabbing hold of my chin and forcing her tongue into my mouth. 'Here, this is a proper birthday surprise.'

'Wow. Just wow,' I said, moving slightly away, feeling both a little astonished and confused.

'I told you. You are a very handsome man. You deserve a nice kiss on your birthday. Maybe even more,' she said.

Eventually, we left the pool and joined Bill for dinner.

'Yes, I saw what was going on. I saw all that hanky-panky,' he said, laughing.

Annie laughed and then winked at me while I decided to say nothing.

'Do I detect young love in the air,' said Sarah as she poured the wine.

'I wouldn't call it love, and I'm certainly not young anymore,' I said,

Annie stared daggers at me across the table. 'What's wrong with falling in love?' she said.

I wasn't sure if Sarah was talking about what I had just said or had just meant it generically. I reached for the wine bottle and almost wrestled the rest of its contents into my glass.

'Plenty of more wine where that came from,' said Bill, raising his glass. 'Happy birthday, Blue Boy,' he chuckled.

'Yes, and here's to love, true love,' said Annie, smiling in my direction.

'How old are you today, Daniel?' asked Sarah.

'People keep asking me lately. I'm forty-six.'

'And what about you? Annie.'

Annie hesitated, and then I saw her wink at Bill. 'I'm twenty-nine' she said.

'Does the age gap worry you,' asked Sarah, looking in Annie's direction.

'No, not all. I prefer mature men, don't I, Bill?'

I looked up from over my dinner fork. Bill looked embarrassed, and Sarah looked confused.

'Besides, it's Daniel I want. We've already been out a couple of times and got on fine.'

'Ah, so it is young love,' said Sarah.

'You'll have to excuse me,' I said. 'I didn't see this coming. It was only a quick snog in the swimming pool.'

'I couldn't hold back any longer,' said Annie. 'That could have happened within an hour or two on the day we met, my lovely.'

'Flipping heck, I didn't notice anything,' I said, feeling rather flattered.

Both Bill and Sarah applauded.

'Daniel, when you learned about my other little vocation, I thought I had ruined it all. You know, ruined my chances of being with you. If you want, I'll stop all that. I want you. I want to spend the rest of my life with you. Here, I'm saying it in front of witnesses.'

Bill rolled his eyes and chuckled again as he reached across the table to grab Sarah's hand.

'Wow. Annie, sorry,' I said. 'I didn't realise how you felt. To be honest, I had thought about us being together. I mean, I considered the age difference but had a lack of belief in myself. Everything was getting in the way. That's why I never said anything.'

'I know, I guessed all that. I could see you were lacking in self-confidence.'

'Was it that obvious?'

'Yes. That's why I felt I had to make the first move. Daniel Blue, I can categorically say I have fallen in love with you.'

Bill and Sarah were applauding even more loudly and cheering this time.

'Congratulations to you both,' said Bill.

'I've never had Bill down as someone I would call Cupid. Stupid, yes, but not Cupid,' said Sarah.

Annie moved around the table to sit beside me.

'Talking of age differences,' said Sarah. 'I have something to say as well. There are over thirty-five years between Bill and me.'

'But you're not an item,' said Annie looking confused.

'Oh yes, we are. When I heard Bill's wife had deserted him, I knew I had to be with Bill.'

'And what about Adonis?' I asked.

'He's history,' said Sarah. 'He really is just history now.'

'That's convenient,' said Annie with a deeply furrowed gaze in Bill's direction.

'Come on. You know me,' said Bill.

'Yes, always the playmaker,' gasped Annie as she filled her glass. 'Here's to love. True love,' she said while squeezing my hand, but clearly agitated by Bill's seemingly new attraction and acquaintance with Sarah.

'Right, you lot,' said Bill. 'Time is getting on. I'll do all the clearing up. Get ready and collect your things. Make sure you have everything. Sarah, are you ready?'

'Yes.'

Sarah kissed Bill on the cheek, grabbed his car keys and drove us off to Portsmouth. Not much was said on the journey, but I did feel a little tension between the two women. Perhaps I was overthinking. I wondered if Annie had become jealous because Sarah had come onto the scene. I also wondered about Sarah's motives. Bill appeared to be a very rich man these days.

After Sarah had dropped us off and we had said our thank yous and goodbyes, I asked Annie what she thought.

'Bill is such a charmer. Even at his age, he can have nearly any woman he wants. He does have that temper, though, and it does let him down. Bill talks before he thinks sometimes. Yes, he likes to flirt, which has cost him his marriage. He reacts like a big baby when things go wrong and feels he needs to cover everything up by swearing. Deep down, he's a very nice man, but not the one for me. You are!'

'And, why me? Honestly. Tell me. I need to know?'

'I think it was love at first sight, if that exists. I don't know. You come across as very sincere, and you smell nice.'

'Smell nice? Is that all?'

'You are very handsome, and I feel comfortable in your company. You treat me like a princess, and you don't take advantage. Yes, I know you have issues. So do I. We can help each other. I know we can.'

'That's very kind.'

‘One question. One big question. Do you love me? Be honest.’

I hesitated, ‘You’re asking me to be honest. Well, let me say I do like you. I like you a lot. The word love frightens me. That said, perhaps I am beginning to love you. I need to remind myself what love is. To fall in love is something I wasn’t expecting.’

‘Yes, sorry. But it’s your birthday. I wanted to give you the best possible present.’

‘And you did, thank you.’

‘Good. Look, my lovely. The ferry is ready for boarding. Let’s go to France, find out what happened to Virna, come back and keep Bill happy and then enjoy the rest of our lives together.’

‘That sounds like a plan.’

‘Let’s do it,’ said Annie, tightening her grip on my hand.

Bill had booked us some comfortable seats on the ferry, which was just as well, as the trip would take twelve hours, arriving in St. Malo at 8.15 in the morning. Annie had nearly fallen asleep, and I could detect a little smile as she rested her head on my shoulder. Her small hand tightly clutched mine as I tried to sort out my head with all that was happening.

Annie then insisted we should upgrade to a cabin, ‘It’s going to be a long night looking out the porthole at a sea of darkness,’ she said. I was apprehensive at first, but it did make sense. So, we ordered some croissants and wine. Getting the cabin also meant we could talk privately and get to know each other a little more. The crossing was rough, so any thought of sleep, or anything more, was cancelled out by what I considered a necessary conversation.

‘I have a confession to make,’ said Annie.

‘Oh dear,’ I said hesitantly but with a smile. ‘What have I let myself in for?’

‘My age. I’m a little older than you think. Quite a lot older, in fact.’

‘How much older?’

‘Eight years.’

‘Flipping heck,’ that would make you...’

‘Thirty-seven, I know. I’m sorry.’

‘So, you’re closer to my age than I thought. You said you were twenty-nine back at Bill’s house.’

'We were having you on. But, yes, there are only nine years in it.'

'Christ, there's no way you look thirty-seven. How do you manage to look so young?'

'Plenty of fruit and vegetables and no red meat. Oh, and I gave up smoking a long time ago.'

'Good!'

'Did I surprise you when I told you I loved you?'

'Yes. Of course. I wasn't expecting that. I had thought about things happening between us, but not love. If I'm honest, I've been having a few erotic dreams of late and was wondering about trying something for real.'

'Did you expect something like that to happen when you came to my place?'

'Sort of, but not quite. To be honest, I was in two minds about what I wanted. I was tempted to allow you to give me a good whipping, but you never offered,' I laughed.

'That's because you are a friend and not a client. As I said, I'm giving all that up now,' said Annie staring into my eyes.

'Just for me?'

'No. Not entirely.'

'Why then?'

'I want to pursue my career as a writer and journalist. There's so much more to explore.'

'Good luck with that. I'm struggling to make ends meet as it is.'

'That's because you're not looking at the big picture. That's exactly why I like Bill, even though, as you said, he "sacked" me once.'

'Why?'

'He will get you a good deal for your story. But not in the way you think.'

'How then?'

'Since you found out about Virna, have you been keeping notes? I mean, like a timeline?'

'Yes, I've been keeping a sort of journal. I've listed all the names of the people I've come across and their locations. I've recorded all the dates and times when certain events took place.

I've even jotted down all the places I've visited. I've still got the receipts from a few.'

'Good, Bill was banking on that. You know you would only get paid a few quid for your story in a newspaper or magazine, right?'

'Bill said it would be a lot more.'

'Not just by submitting it to a newspaper or magazine, it won't be. Look, my lovely, and this is where I come in. Yes, I can proofread and edit. I'm a qualified copyeditor, for God's sake. I'm also a ghost-writer.'

'Ghost-writer?'

'Yes. Bill has suggested that I help you turn your story into a book. He wants you to call it, The Story of Virna Babineaux.'

'What?'

'Yes, he knows a lot of publishers and agents in the book publishing world. He's even got contacts in Hollywood. He's already got a couple lined up. You could be the next Lee Child!'

'Ha, ha, I've never written a book in my life.'

'Listen to me. We'll sit down and review all your notes, and I'll transcript the story for you.'

'As in a novel?'

'Yes. It'll be based on the true story of how Virna's body went missing from the morgue.'

'There's one problem with that. We don't even know if that's what happened ourselves.'

'And that's why this trip is so important. Aren't you feeling confident?'

'Not as much as I would like to. There's been too many knockbacks and false hopes already.'

'And procrastination. That's why I'm here to help.'

'Thank you.'

'If we can find and talk to Jonathan Blackwell, we'll solve the mystery.'

'I hope so. What if Jonathan doesn't want to talk?'

'Then I'll use my powers of persuasion. I saw him described somewhere as a bit of a ladies' man. I'll smile sweetly at him and loosen my blouse.'

'What?'

'It's alright, my lovely. I'm only playing with you.'

‘Ha, ha, very funny. Anyway, shouldn’t we be getting some sleep? We have a long day ahead of us tomorrow.’

24

'Bonjour, mesdames et messieurs, c'est le capitaine qui parle. Veuillez noter que nous arriverons au port de St Malo dans une vingtaine de minutes. Assurez-vous d'avoir tous vos effets personnels avec vous avant de débarquer. L'équipage et moi-même tenons à vous remercier d'avoir choisi Brittany Ferries. Veuillez poursuivre votre voyage en toute sécurité.'

'What did he say?'

'Be patient, my lovely. Listen, the captain will repeat it in English.'

'Good morning, ladies and gentlemen. This is the captain speaking. Please be advised that we will arrive at the port of St Malo in approximately twenty minutes. Please ensure you have all your belongings with you before disembarking. The crew and I would like to thank you for choosing Brittany Ferries. Please have a safe onward journey.'

'Ah, I can see you've done this all before.'

'It's usual for the captain to speak in both languages. It's refreshing that it's not automated. The message always sounds more sincere when it's a human-being speaking,' said Annie, hurriedly searching for her make-up bag.

'So, what's the plan today?'

'After we leave the boat, we will find our hotel for the night. They probably won't let us check in straight away, but we should be able to dump our bags there before we go walkabouts.'

'Just a minute, which hotel?'

'I don't remember. Oh, it's this one,' said Annie showing me the receipt on her phone.'

'Three stars? Fucking cheap skate. No wonder he's so bloody rich.'

'Ha, ha. Don't worry. Bill's also given me 500 Euros if we want to upgrade. It should be easy enough to find something decent this time of year. Anyway, this hotel has a nice penthouse suite. We could see if that's available.'

'I hope so.'

'Ha, ha. Surprise. I know so.'

‘How? Have you been here before?’

‘No, but I’m a woman, and women do their homework. Calm down. I had a little search on the internet while we were on the ferry.’

‘Oh, Google to the rescue yet again!’

‘You could say that.’

It didn’t take too long to leave the ferry, and it was a short walk into the town of St Malo itself. I was impressed by the cobbled streets and all the architecture.

‘Quaint, isn’t it, my lovely?’

‘It is. Isn’t that bread I can smell baking?’

‘Probably, it could be croissants. I love croissants.’

‘Yes, I know. You ate enough on the ferry.’

‘Cheeky,’ said Annie with a smile.

We both smiled broadly and then embraced each other with a tight hug and a kiss.

‘Listen, let’s get to the hotel. It should be just around the corner. Then we can find somewhere to sit down and have a coffee. Have a good chat and everything. Let’s get to know each other even more.’

‘Sounds good to me.’

We turned the corner into Place Chateaubriand, and there it was, the Hôtel de l’Univers.

‘Lovely old place, isn’t it?’ said Annie reaching for her phone. ‘Let me take a couple of pictures.’

‘Ah, les amoureux de l'anglais. Laissez-moi prendre une photo de vous deux ensemble,’ said an elderly woman as she approached us.

‘The lady has offered to photograph us both,’ said Annie.

‘Oh right, I wondered what she said.’

The woman took around four photos on Annie’s smartphone. Annie offered her some euros, but she refused to take any money and quickly disappeared into a shop on the other side of the road.

‘There, it’s there for all to see. We’re officially an item,’ said Annie laughing. ‘Come on, let’s check in and drop our bags off.’

The receptionist was very friendly and spoke good English, telling us he lived in Bagshot for a few years back in the 1990s. He said we could go to our room immediately as no-one had been staying the previous night. By now, it was 10 a.m. Annie ordered a bottle of prosecco for the room, ensuring I realised it was strictly for later.

'I don't want to change you, my lovely. But if I can help you curtail your drinking habits, that would be good. Let's treat this as a working holiday and enjoy ourselves. Even I need alcohol to let my hair down properly.'

'Excuse me, I'm already curtailing my drinking,' I said, smiling. I wasn't sure if I was misreading Annie's intentions or not.

'Sorry, that came out a little wrong. I didn't mean to be so condescending.'

'Forget it, don't worry,' I said, trying not to make a big thing of it.

After stepping out of the hotel, we found a cafe called Le rire de Lenny.

'Laughing Lenny's,' said Annie. The whole place is dedicated to Leonard Cohen. You can hear his music all day long and even buy a tee shirt. The French love him. He died a few years ago.'

'Yes, I know, November 2016, to be precise. My old dad loved him too.'

'Here, though, it should be cosy enough to sit and have a proper chat. I'll order a couple of coffees.'

'Great, thanks,' I said, preparing myself for a frank conversation.

'Are you sure you're okay, my lovely?'

'Err, yes. Well, I think so. I'm still a little perplexed by the fact that we seem to have suddenly become an item, almost overnight, so to speak.'

'Sorry. No, I'm not sorry. Are you happy?'

'Yes. I didn't expect it, that's all. Though I have to ask, what attracted you to me?'

'You have an honest vulnerability about you. As I've already said, you are handsome and smell nice. Besides, you are not judgemental. You accept people for who they are, and as I already know, you do not take advantage.'

'And that's it?'

'It's enough, isn't it?'

'If you say so.'

'May I ask, my lovely, what attracted you to me?'

‘Firstly, your flowing red hair and your beautiful green eyes. Then there was the mystique. My imagination was running wild. When we first met, my mental health was going downhill fast. You’re right. The alcohol wasn’t helping, but in a roundabout way, it had. Now I drink less and feel better about it. It’s under control, and that’s the main thing. I can go days without a drink now if I want to.’

‘That’s good. How did you feel when you discovered I was a part-time dominatrix?’

‘I didn’t want to believe it. I was looking for something to spice up my sex life after Sue had buggered off. After all, I’m in my mid-forties and wanted to experiment, you know, experience something more than a quick, wham-bam-thank-you-mam.’

‘What, shag?’

‘Yes, I suppose so.’

‘That sounds a little shallow.’

‘I called it a mid-life crisis. I was beginning to have all these fantasies and erotic dreams. Strangely, I felt some comfort just dreaming about things.’

‘Then you met me. Oh, oh, my lovely. Did you want to make love to me?’

‘I’ll be brutally honest. The thought did cross my mind until you told me about being a virgin prostitute, as you put it.’

‘Ha, ha. I always found that was a unique way of describing myself to people in the know. Remember, I’ve never had sex with any of my clients. There is no physical contact whatsoever, not even a kiss.’

‘So how do the men get off just by being whipped?’

‘They just do. Now, haven’t I told you all this before?’

I grinned. ‘You have. Now, just one question.’

‘What, my lovely?’

‘Sorry, I have to ask, was Bill one of your clients?’

‘In a way, yes, in a way, no.’ I simply used to tease him, that’s all. For some reason, he never wanted to take his trousers down.’

‘Why?’

‘Something embarrassed him. He also talked about his wife a lot, and I think his conscience stopped him from going further. Plus, I was working with him professionally, so it wasn’t what you would call ethical. I was never comfortable with it, but one thing is for sure.'

'What?'

'It's fair to say he always made me laugh and paid me handsomely.'

'And now he has Sarah.'

'Yes, but that won't last. Bill is missing his wife too much. Trust me, I know.'

Another question, sorry. When was the last time you had proper sex? If you don't mind me asking.'

'You mean intercourse?' said Annie, pensively.

'Yes.'

'About five years ago. I was in love, well, if it was love. A merchant banker guy called Isaac. Wow, he was rich!'

'Richer than Bill?'

I don't know about that. Isaac had just left his wife and two kids. Then it all went wrong.'

'How?'

'One of the boys had an awful accident at school and wasn't expected to live. He survived but needed round-the-clock treatment. Isaac returned to his wife to help, which was the end of that. He even blanks me in the street if he sees me now. It's almost as if I don't exist.'

'Sorry.'

'Don't be, my lovely. I'm guessing the last time you had sex was with that police lady you were seeing?'

'Sue, yes.'

'How long ago was that?'

'I can't remember,' I said, while choosing not to tell Annie about my last close encounter with Sue.

'Do you think she will come back for you?'

I hesitated. 'Not when she finds out I'm with someone new.'

'Good, and she had better not.'

'About the dominatrix thing. Are you sure you want to give it up?'

'Yes, my lovely. I've had some fun and made a bit of money, but morality has now got the better of me. I need to settle down and get on with my writing career. Besides, I'm with you now, so it's all onwards and upwards.'

'I like that.'

'And so you should. Let's see if we can find this Jonathan chap before time gets the better of us.'

'So, where do we start?'

'First, I want to visit the Robert Surcouf statue. I'm intrigued. It should give us a good starting point. Then, let's find out where all the British ex-pats go. There must be a place around here like that somewhere. We should find someone who may know where Jonathan lives.'

The statue is near the beach, and the figure of Robert Surcouf is pointing north towards England. A plaque near the statue reads Robert Surcouf (12 December 1773–8 July 1827) and states he was a famous French corsair.

During his legendary career, he captured forty-seven ships and was renowned for his gallantry and chivalry, earning the Roi des Corsaires (King of Corsairs) nickname.

'Impressive. Exactly what we saw on the internet,' said Annie. 'It looks like it's recently had a makeover.'

'I still wonder why Virna's killer named himself after him,' I said. 'I don't think he had any connection with St Malo.'

'I think the location is just an odd coincidence. As you've already found out, he was fascinated with Surcouf, besotted even. He must have been to take the name as a non-de-plume.'

As we talked, a guy with a guitar approached us and asked if we knew where the Le rire de Lenny cafe was.

'That's strange. We've just come from there. It's only around the corner,' said Annie, pointing.

'I'm playing there later; I have a live slot with some other guys.'

'What songs do you play?'

'I play anything. Tonight, I am performing some Leonard Cohen songs.'

'Can you play one for us now?' asked Annie excitedly.

'What here?'

'Yes, here,' she almost demanded.

'Which song?'

'I don't think we know any,' I said, 'it was my father who was a big fan.'

'Is your father no longer with us?'

'No, unfortunately not.'

'Then, I will dedicate this song to him. It's called Suzanne. It's quite a famous one.'

Suzanne takes you down to her place near the river You can hear the boats go by, you can spend the night beside her...

'Wow, that's just beautiful. Please, please carry on,' said Annie, wiping a tear from her eye.

'If you want to hear the rest of it and some other songs. Come along to the cafe later. I might even let you buy me a drink. I'm Pierre, by the way.'

'Thank you, Pierre. We'll try and catch you later,' I said.

By now, a crowd had gathered. As we walked away, Pierre began singing the rest of the song and some more of his repertoire. We paused.

'That's Bowie's The Man Who Sold the World, isn't it?' I said.

'I don't know,' said Annie, tugging on my arm and pointing to a small poster in the window of what looked like a bar, 'Look, St Malo Britons, this looks like a place all the ex-pats might come to.'

Indeed, as we entered, all we could hear were English voices.

'Haven't seen you guys in here before,' said the waitress with a broad northern accent. 'Where are you from?'

'Basically, we're here from Surrey. It's what you might call a flying visit. We go back on the ferry on Monday,' said Annie.

'Honeymoon?' said the waitress, winking.

'No, nothing like that. We're over here trying to find an artist called Jonathan. Would you know him?'

'Artist? Is he British?'

'Yes,' I said.

An elderly man with a long white beard then interrupted the conversation.

'I'm an artist. Which artist are you looking for? I know a couple of Jonathans, and they're both from England.'

'Jonathan Blackwell,' said Annie. 'Do you know where we can find him?'

'Are you his daughter?' asked the old man.

'No, nothing like that. We're great admirers of his work, though, aren't we, Daniel.'

'Yes, it would be nice to catch up with him. Can you tell us where he lives?' I asked.

'No, no, no,' said the old man. 'I can't do that. You could be anyone.'

'I understand,' said Annie. 'But he is here in St Malo, right?'

'Yes. Look, if you want to find Jonnie, there is a Christmas exhibition tomorrow at the cathedral. It'll be after the morning mass. You will find him there.'

'Thank you, thank you,' shrieked Annie excitedly.

'Can I buy you a beer or something?' I asked.

'Of course, I'm Solomon by the way, Solomon Smith, those are my prints on the wall.'

'Abstracts?' I said quizzically.

'Yes, abstracts of nude ladies. It's those pictures which pay my bar tab.'

'You are very talented,' said Annie.

'We all are. It's a shame that the French appreciate our artwork more than the British. The funny thing is that nearly every British tourist takes some of our work back with them. Oh, the irony!' he laughed.

'Very ironic,' said the waitress as she brought us more beers.

'Look, Daniel, my lovely, time is getting on, and we haven't had dinner yet. Shall we find a restaurant?'

'We can go back to the hotel and eat, can't we?'

'Yes, then we go back to the cafe and listen to that guitar player. Did he say what his name was?'

'Yes, Pierre.'

'Oh, that's it. He was very good.'

'He was. My old dad would have loved him,' I said, feeling a lump in my throat.

The evening was a very poignant one. One I will never forget. The meal we had at the restaurant was what Annie described as 'divine', and then the event at the cafe was brilliant. Pierre and a couple of other performers played some Leonard Cohen songs and then played some requests for the audience near the end. It was a small, intimate, and friendly affair. It was like meeting a bunch of new friends all in one go. Annie loved it.

We then went back to the hotel room. Annie and I stood by the window. We locked eyes with each other. It was the first time I had felt nervous during the whole weekend.

'I love you, Mr Blue!'

I was staring, admiring, wondering. It was a surreal moment and one I didn't want to end.

'I love you too, now, there, I've said it.'

Annie smiled. There I was with a woman who I could fully describe as beautiful. I felt I was the luckiest man on earth.

'What now?' asked Annie.

I guess our eyes had been doing the talking for us. I then softened the light as we slowly undressed—Annie's blouse, my shirt, essentially sharing the responsibility to remove each garment as we ritualistically explored each other with an almost choreographed seduction.

And then, there we were. The lovers. Naked. Spreadeagled and entwined on the vast bed, lost in each other's eyes. After a long silence, Annie rose like a serpent and reached down for my penis as I fervently kissed the pout nipple of her right breast and then, slowly, the left.

She whispered something in French into my ear, and I felt my penis get hard. I mean, really hard. She pulled her hair back and placed her beautiful body, with its pale and shapely thighs, on top of me, pushing my penis deep inside her. Her eyes were still locked on mine. She lowered her mouth towards my lips, and then we kissed. I moved slowly up and then down, up and down, until we rolled over.

'Make love to me. Come on, yes. Please come inside me. Yes, yes. Oh, Daniel. Fuck me!'

I wasn't expecting Annie to swear, but her voice had a certain sincerity about it. I knew this was more than just a fuck. It really did feel like making love!

'Oh, Daniel, Daniel.'

As she screamed my name, I felt myself jerking and gyrating in some breathless orgasmic rhythm routine. Something I had never felt before.

'Oh, Daniel, yes, yes.'

And then it happened. That HALLELUJAH moment as we writhed to the point of ecstasy, tightening and squeezing our bodies even closer together.

That was the precise moment I knew all life's anxieties had been released. That incredible moment where true love presents itself and conquers all, and you know one special person has come along and changed your life forever.

'Oh my, oh my. What are you thinking?' asked Annie.

'I think you can guess,' I said rather sheepishly.

'Yes, and I love you too, you handsome bugger. You are a master of love-making, aren't you!'

If only she knew, I thought.

'Thank you for loving me, my lovely,' she laughed.

'And thank you for being you.'

It was a magical night, and Annie was a wonderful woman. I felt her turn on her side. Then there was perfect silence. I just had to stay awake and watch her sleeping in the moonlight.

The next thing, dawn was breaking through the hotel shutters.

25

At breakfast, everything was quiet, no conversation whatsoever, just the clink of a coffee cup on a saucer as Annie gazed out of the window while I summoned the waiter.

'More coffee?' he asked.

'Yes, please.' I said, hoping Annie would join the conversation. I wasn't sure what was going through her head, so I waited for her to speak first. It seemed like an eternity.

Eventually, she turned towards me and smiled. 'Thank you,' she said.

'Thank you for what?'

'For last night. For being so kind and gentle.'

'Sorry, I don't understand?'

'You made love to me, didn't you?' she whispered.

'Well, yes.'

'That, my lovely, is what I'm thanking you for.'

'Oh.'

'It was beautiful. I'm sorry I fell asleep.'

'We both did that. I know I did eventually. I hope I didn't disappoint?'

'No, no, you didn't. I thought I may have disappointed you. I will show you what I can really do next time.'

'That sounds daunting.'

'Girls have fantasies too, you know.'

'Which is why I suppose you wanted to become a dominatrix?'

'Shoosh, yes, if I'm honest. It is!'

'Does that mean I'm due for a good whipping next?'

Annie laughed. 'Only if you want me to. I know I have so much more to give.'

'Like what?'

'I want to discover more of you and what you like.'

'How?'

'Foreplay,' said Annie, reaching out to touch my face.

'Flipping heck.'

'Yes, my lovely. Foreplay. Masturbation and oral, for instance. And what about tantric? I love it.'

'Mm.'

'There would have been more pressure on you last night. First-time nerves with someone new and all that. I felt it too, my lovely.'

'Yes, I do know.'

'And we did make out. It was beautiful.'

'It was,' I said, feeling relieved and grateful.

'Remember, I haven't had what you call proper sex for such a long time, and I miss all those things.'

'Then it's a shame we're not staying here at the hotel later,' I said.

'Don't worry. The ferry cabin will have to do. We also have a whole lifetime ahead of us now, don't we?'

'Yes, I suppose we have.'

'Then at least sound a little more positive about it.'

I laughed.

'Come on, my lovely, let's get moving. We can leave our bags here and collect them later on the way back to the ferry port. Let's go to the cathedral and find this Jonathan guy.'

It was now just after ten o'clock, and the congregation was slowly leaving. So far, as cathedrals go, it was fairly small compared to many of the others I had previously visited, such as Sacré-Coeur and Notre Dame in Paris. St Malo Cathedral is a quant 12th-century building with a simple spire.

Annie was panicking as she couldn't see any sign of an art exhibition, so we went back to the ex-pats' bar to see if we could find anything out. The place was packed. We could see a couple of retro-Volkswagen camper vans parked outside, and Annie pointed out some artwork she had seen on a back seat.

'Let's gently push our way through and ask what's going on,' she said.

The woman behind the bar remembered us from yesterday. 'They always come in for a cosy drink before going to the church,' she said. 'Give it until about midday, and then things will start to happen. Here, have a beer each on me.'

'Thank you,' I said. 'Do you know if Jonathan Blackwell is here at the moment?'

‘No, he usually comes in afterwards with his lady friend.’

‘You don’t happen to know her name, do you,’ asked Annie, not missing the opportunity.’

‘Actually, I don’t. She’s quite a pretty woman for her age. She comes from Paris, I believe. Somehow, her name escapes me.’

‘It wouldn’t be Virna, would it?’ I asked.

‘Shoosh,’ whispered Annie, ‘We don’t want to be asking any more questions about her yet, remember!’

Fortunately, I don’t think the woman behind the bar heard me. We stayed, had a couple of beers, and then walked back to the cathedral.

‘That’s better. I can see some artists setting up now.’ Annie said excitedly.

There was a group of men and women of all ages. Most were French, some were English, and we could hear some Italian-speaking artists.

‘Look up there,’ said Annie.

On the wall were nine paintings, three at the top, three in the middle and three at the bottom: nudes, ballerinas and clowns, all signed by Jonathan Blackwell.

‘Bingo!’ gasped Annie. ‘We’ve found him.’

‘Not quite,’ I said, aware there was no sign of anyone who looked like Jonathan.

Just then, a woman wearing a red head scarf approached us. ‘Bonjour, aimez-vous ces peintures?’

‘Hi,’ I said, not understanding a word.

‘Ils sont tous de mon ami Jonnie Blackwell. Veux-tu acheter?’

‘Bonjour, est-ce que l'artiste est là?’ said Annie.

‘Ah, are you English?’ said the woman. ‘He’s gone for a pee-pee.’

We laughed and then waited. Annie was nervously clutching my hand. One of the paintings was like one I had seen hanging on the wall at Virna’s house in Knaphill. I was beginning to feel very excited.

Just then, a voice barked from behind us.

‘Mr Daniel Blue, the intrepid reporter, I’ve been expecting you, Jonathan Charles Blackwell, at your service.’ he said, removing his beanie hat, revealing a bald scalp.

At last, we had found Jonathan, a relatively short man in his early to mid-seventies. He was wearing a blue denim jacket, a grey University of Kent sweatshirt and avocado-coloured corduroy trousers. He greeted us with a curious smile but seemed a little apprehensive at the same time.

'How come you were expecting me?' I asked.

'Because I have friends.'

'Friends?'

'Yes, in Portland. I got a call from a good friend who still lives there. I was told a reporter called Blue was looking for me. Then a few weeks later, the same thing happened, a call from my dainty Irish friend, Kathy, who runs a pub on the Isle of Wight.'

'The Vyne?'

'In Freshwater, yes. Okay, look, I know exactly what you want to speak about. Give me a minute. I'll ask Fabienne to watch my work.'

Annie looked shocked. I think she was hoping the woman with Jonathan would be Virna. There was a stark similarity, but I soon convinced myself we wouldn't be that lucky.

'Come on, let's go to Laughing Lenny's. We can talk there without too much interruption,' said Jonathan, gesturing with his hands.

'And you will tell us what you know?' asked Annie.

'Of course,' said Jonathan.

When we got to the café, it was clear Jonathan was quite well known.

'I have an account here. I half live in this place,' he said whilst beckoning the waitress.

'We were here yesterday, weren't we, Daniel?' said Annie.

'Oh, the Leonard Cohen gig thing, I nearly came with Fabienne, but we had too many vinos over dinner.'

'Good for you,' said Annie, trying to break the ice.

'So, I gather you want to talk to me about Virna Babineaux?'

'Yes. I was alerted to a story about some strange goings on at Virna's house in Knaphill. Things then spiralled from there,' I said.

'I can tell you that I owned the house. I sold it only last month. It was becoming a burden, and I needed the extra money to supplement my pension. Living out here is getting more expensive than you can imagine.'

'You can say that again,' said Annie. 'It's bad enough back home.'

'I'm sure it is. Now, let me tell you about Virna.'

'Thank you,' said Annie, reaching for my hand.

'Back in 2010, we were lovers. She was a lot younger than me, but we had delicious sex all the same. The trouble was that her career as a model was failing as she grew older. I mean, all the work was drying up. One day, she discovered she could make a lot of money by becoming a high-class prostitute. Most of her clients were Arabs, and she was duping them into paying up to five grand a trick. On the back of that, an old boyfriend of hers became very jealous and showed up on the scene like a bad penny.'

'Robert Surcouf?' I asked.

'Ah, Gross, yes, but Surcouf was what he called himself. Anyway, he caused a big rift between us.'

'We heard,' said Annie.

'We had a big fight. It was then I told Virna she could live in the house as long as she wanted, and I shot off to Portland, but only after I thought Gross, or rather, Surcouf was out of both of our lives for good.'

'What about your wife? Where does she fit into all this?' I asked.

'Wife? No, please. Leave Jilly out of this. I don't want to talk about her anymore.'

'Okay, sorry about that. We didn't mean to pry,' I said.

'Good,' snapped Jonathan, appearing a little agitated.

'Well, then. Let's get back to Virna,' said Annie.

'The weird thing was. I didn't know Virna had been murdered until two years after the event, so when I found out, I assumed there had already been a funeral. Fabienne, who you just met, is Virna's eldest cousin. She's the best part of three years younger than Virna. As she hadn't heard anything for such a long time, she started to enquire about her whereabouts, then finally tracked me down on the Isle of Wight in 2019, some seven years after Virna had been killed. I'm still unsure how, but Fabienne and I have been an item ever since.'

‘You must have something about you the ladies like,’ I said.

‘I’ve always been lucky with the chicks. Even now, I have trouble fighting them off.’

‘Self-flattery,’ said Annie. ‘It’ll get you nowhere.’

‘I beg to differ,’ said Jonathan, raising his glass with a big smile.

‘Come on, please, let’s be serious for a minute,’ said Annie. ‘How did you originally find out about the murder?’

‘I saw an old magazine article about Gross, or rather, Surcouf taking his own life in a prison cell. After putting two and two together, I then went back to Knaphill and spoke with Iona, the neighbour. Iona agreed to watch the house for me and keep it clean and tidy, almost as if someone was still living there. I thought it would keep the vandals away. Remember, it would have been empty for the two years immediately after Virna died. It was lucky the place was still relatively intact.’

‘So, you’re saying that Iona was responsible for all the strange stuff happening at the house?’ I asked.

‘Yes, well. I’m not sure what you mean by strange stuff, but I paid Iona fifty quid a month to keep her eye on things. She’s been doing so since the summer of 2014.’

‘Flipping heck, that’s strange as it was her who alerted the police about things in the first place,’ I said.

‘There was always something a little odd about that woman. I could never fathom her out,’ said Jonathan, taking a sip from his glass before ordering another bottle of wine.

‘Red, okay?’

‘Yes, please,’ said Annie.

‘Good. Let me explain,’ said Jonathan, looking shamelessly down at Annie’s cleavage. ‘When Virna died, she was still using her professional identity. Her real name was Veronique Guyot. That’s what all her childhood friends and family knew her as here in France. British records had her down as Babineaux. French records had her as Guyot. From a very young age, she always had a dual identity.’

‘I understand that Babineaux was the name on her French passport though,’ I said.

‘Oh yes, it was. She never liked calling herself Guyot, but she did use it sometimes as a means to an end,’ said Jonathan.

'Actually,' said Annie. 'Daniel and I had already discovered Virna's real name a while ago. Could this be why her body was kept in the morgue so long?'

'Ah, a rather unfortunate mix-up over the name. Almost certainly. It's probably why the authorities think the body went missing. It didn't,' said Jonathan, laughing.

'Why are you laughing?' I said, a little surprised at his reaction.

'Virna's family had been talking to the French cops, who passed the case on to Europol. After a while, some evidence was recovered from the original murder inquiry and DNA tests were carried out. A London copper called Jim Green eventually contacted me, and arrangements were made for Virna's body to be released from the morgue for burial. I managed to trace and contact an old friend of Virna's called Helena, and she was able to fill me in with all the gory details.'

'Helena Cieslak?' I asked.

'Yes, thanks to her, we got things moving, and Fabienne made the formal identification at the mortuary. We flew back with the body to Paris.'

'When was this?' asked Annie.

'September 2020.'

'During Covid?'

'Yes. Virna is now at peace in a small churchyard in Antony near where she grew up. She's been there for nearly two years now. Fabienne and her sisters planted a small pink rosebush on her grave.'

'That's so lovely. Rest in Peace, Virna,' said Annie, wiping a tear from her eye.

'Unbelievably, I've met Helena during my inquiries a couple of times. She never told me any of this,' I said. 'In fact, she's lied through her teeth.'

'This Helena chick was Virna's best friend for a long while. She's always been very loyal towards her,' said Jonathan.

'The policeman, Jim Green. What do you remember about him?' I asked.

'Ah yes, a very shifty character. I wouldn't trust him so far as I could throw him,' said Jonathan.

‘His name came up for various reasons during the early part of my investigation. Why didn’t he tell someone that he had found the answer?’ I asked.

‘Negligence at the very least,’ said Annie.

‘Corrupt, I suspect. Fuck, there has to be a reason. Not only does it appear that Jim bloody Green instigated the body’s removal, but it also looks like he covered everything up when he was supposedly investigating it!’ I said.

‘And I know exactly why,’ said Jonathan. ‘He was bribed. Virna’s family, they are all cousins by the way, gave him a couple of grand to stay quiet.’

‘Just cousins?’ asked Annie.

‘Yes. Apparently, they were the only family Virna had left. Anyway, they didn’t want her memory besmirched anymore. It was their way of ensuring that Veronique, as they still continue to call her, was finally laid to rest without any more unwanted attention. Essentially, I’m trying to tell you that Virna’s body was removed from the mortuary under the name of Veronique Guyot. Jim Green arranged it all with Europol.’

‘In such a way, the records were never updated at the morgue,’ I said.

‘I can’t believe Jim Green has so blatantly interfered with the inquiry,’ said Annie.

‘All about money. Now it’s off my chest at least,’ said Jonathan.

‘No doubt about that,’ I said. ‘What a ….’

‘Now, now,’ said Annie. ‘Calm down. It’s a long road which has no turnings. We’ll make sure Mr Green gets his comeuppance!’

‘I hope so,’ I said, quickly recomposing myself.

‘You two must understand that I need to safeguard Fabienne. You know, although she’s in her fifties, she’s a lot younger than me and still quite sensitive about everything. She overthinks too much. I’ve had to tell you all this out of her earshot. She doesn’t like it all being brought back. Virna and Fabienne were more like sisters.’

‘You’ve just answered my next question. I was thinking that,’ said Annie.

‘Anything else?’ asked Jonathan.

‘I remember Robert Surcouf wasn’t recorded under his real name of Gross when he went for trial. Do you think there is there some kind of lapse with Europol’s data when it comes to this sort of thing?’ I asked. ‘I mean, it all seems a bit odd, doesn’t it?

‘Almost certainly,’ said Jonathan. ‘The French, in general, are very incompetent, and it appears those working for Europol were no exception. We found a loophole and adopted a ploy of simple ignorance to get Virna’s body back here to France. It worked a treat.’

‘Is there any way we can corroborate your story?’ asked Annie.

‘Corroborate? Probably not unless you can get Jim Green to cough the lot. Perhaps you might be able to bribe him too.’

‘Don’t worry. I have connections. A certain DI should be able to do that for me,’ I said, thinking of Sue.

‘I’m sure we’ll get to the truth in the end,’ said Annie.

‘I’ve just bloody well told you both the whole truth, everything. Is that it?’

‘Yes, yes, you have. Thank you, Jonathan. Just one question, though. Can you tell us what *Fugazi* means?’ I asked.

Jonathan looked bemused. ‘*Fugazi*? Where did you get that from?’

‘It’s an inscription on the back of all your paintings I saw at the house back in Knaphill.’

‘Do you really want to know?’ he said, rolling his eyes and scratching his head.

‘Yes, please!’ said Annie. ‘Daniel is keen to know what it means.’

‘It means, “All fucked up.” It’s a Japanese word, and my relationship with Virna was certainly that. Fucked up, I mean. The weird thing was, we both knew it! It’s all very ironic now, don’t you think?’

‘Why ironic?’

‘I sent those paintings to Virna shortly after we split. I knew how much she loved them. Despite everything, I was still in love with her, but I didn’t agree with the new life she had chosen for herself.’

‘As a prostitute,’ said Annie.

'Yes. I was leaving those paintings to Virna, thinking that because of my age, I would die first. We were always a bit of an odd couple. We tried to keep our relationship low profile, despite always being in the limelight, hence, *Fugazi*. We loved each other immensely, but things just weren't just working out. The real irony is that Virna was the first to pop her clogs.'

'Much before her time. Poor you,' I said.

'No, poor Virna. At least I have Fabienne now.'

'Jonathan, thank you for your time,' said Annie. 'We do appreciate it. Is there anything else you can tell us?'

'No. I think you have it all. You've plucked the very sinews of my emotions too much already.'

'Sorry,' said Annie, 'we did notice you were getting a little emotional, didn't we Daniel?'

'Yes, sorry,' I said, reaching out to shake his hand.

'Don't be. I've told you everything. Now, fuck off back to Blighty and leave me alone,' Jonathan said with a big smile.

'I liked him,' said Annie as we left the café and walked towards the hotel to collect our bags.

'That's because he's a serial womaniser. I saw him looking at your tits.'

'Now, now. You're jealous!'

'What of an old man?'

'Ha, ha. Come on, my lovely. You'll be like that one day.'

'Then let's hope you're still around to look after me.'

'You're funny. Let's phone Bill and tell him the great news.'

'What news?'

'That we finally have the story of Virna Babineaux, Stupid!'

'Oh, that news,' I said as we skipped along the street like a couple of excitable teenage kids.

'STOP!' said Annie, assertively.

'What?'

'Listen. It's Pierre. He's down there by the statue singing our song.'

Now, Suzanne takes your hand, and she leads you to the river,
She is wearing rags and feathers from Salvation Army counters.

‘Our song? I like that.’
‘Shoosh, said Annie, let him finish.’

And you want to travel with her, and you want to travel blind,
And then you know that you can trust her
For she's touched your perfect body with her mind.

‘Beautiful, isn’t it, my lovely?’
For once, I felt lost for words, but yes, beautiful, it certainly was. Now though, it was time for the next chapter in my life. Flipping heck! Where the hell is that going to take me?

Milton Keynes UK
Ingram Content Group UK Ltd.
UKHW020652031023
429857UK00019B/155